mystory

Don Summerhayes

mystory

Don Summerhayes

TORONTO

Exile Editions
1997

This edition is published by Exile Editions Limited,
20 Dale Avenue, Toronto, Ontario, Canada   M4W 1K4

Sales Distribution:
General Distribution Services
30 Lesmill Road
Don Mills, ON
M3B 2T6
1-800-387-0172

Composition and Design by MICHAEL P. CALLAGHAN
Typeset at MOONS OF JUPITER, TORONTO
Printed and Bound by AMPERSAND PRINTING, GUELPH
Author's Photograph by MERLIN HOMER
Cover Design by MICHAEL P. CALLAGHAN

Grateful acknowledgement is made to *Exile: The Literary Quarterly* (Vol. 20, No. 4, Fall 1997) and *Smoke: A Journal of Literary Prose* (Vol 1, No. 1, Summer 1997), in which sections of this text appeared.

The publisher wishes to acknowledge
the assistance toward publication of
the Canada Council and the Ontario Arts Council.

The Canada Council

ISBN 1-55096-172-1

For Pearl Karal
And for Merlin Homer always

ONE

1. (self), *n. pl.* **selves,** *adj. pron. pl.* **selves.** – *n.* **1.** a person or thing referred to with respect to individuality; one's own person: *one's own self.* **2.** one's nature, character, etc.: *one's better self.* **3.** personal interest; selfishness. **4.** *Philos.* the individual consciousness in its relation to itself. [ME and OE, c. D *zelf,* G *selb*]

2. I got up at six, showered, made a cup of instant coffee and took it up to my study on the third floor of the house, where I settled down at the table in the east window to write. Almost every day I wrote in a series of journals I had picked up in a Dollar Store, buying twenty against what was suddenly an urge for bulk, for a lot of words. I was writing not for eventual publication but as a kind of evacuation, getting out thoughts and memories that otherwise merely fed my chronic depression. I wanted to testify. It was raw writing, starting as much as possible arbitrarily and going by random association or linkage of some kind not calculated until about seven-thirty, when I went to the Y for a swim, and then drove up to the university for my first class at ten. I did this faithfully for twenty-four months, through eight seasons, starting my official job with the feeling that I had already put in a useful day's work. With the help of my therapist, Pearl, one morning a week for an hour, this regimen eventually brought me out of the misery I had thought was to be my condition for the rest of my life. Strangely, I never considered suicide.

3. My Grandma went out to two families, the Keaghies and another whose name I probably never knew. She did for them. She had stopped with the other family when I first found about it, and just had the Keaghies, where she went on Thursdays, for the whole day from soon after breakfast until she had finished the supper dishes. They lived at the edge of the Park, behind a low stone wall, on a wide deep lot that had crab apple trees and willows with branches

down to the ground, and gardens all around the gray stone cottage where my Grandma went in the back door to do her work.

4. Before the first white men penetrated Ontario's forests, the Dundas area was occupied by the Neutral tribe of Indians, so called because they took no part in the battles between the Hurons to the north and the Senecas of New York State. In 1649, the Senecas utterly defeated the Hurons, and in 1650 vanquished the Neutrals, so that these two Indian groups never again existed as separate tribes.

The Senecas occupied these conquered territories for a time, but they gradually withdrew southward toward their former home, and as they with drew, the Mississagas from the Manitoulin area infiltrated their hunting grounds. Consequently, when the first white settlers were sent into the Niagara Peninsula, it was the Mississagas who occupied the land. The British Government has always recognized the rights of Indians by buying the land from them. For instance, Britain bought the Niagara Peninsula on May 22, 1784, so that she would have land to give to the settlers that were beginning to penetrate the Canadian wilderness. [*The History of the Town of Dundas*, Part One, 4]

5. Only reading loves the work, maintains with it a relation of desire. To read is to desire the work, to want to be the work, to refuse to double the work outside any word other than that of the work itself. The only commentary that a true reader could produce and that would remain so, is the pastiche (as would be indicated by the example of Proust, lover of both readings and pastiches). [Roland Barthes, *Critique et verité*, 78-79]

6. His tolerance, even affection, for bits of himself, *excrementia*: hair in the brush, fingernails and toenails, snot on the tissue, hangnails, scabs, tweezed beard hair, even the shit in the toilet bowl, that he never failed to inspect. Alice Notley: In the morning, when you get up, your body is already there for you.

7. To redeem the text from the false order of chronology, it is only necessary to redistribute its parts, unsystematically — as a kind of metaphor for the activity of simultaneous systems of memory, observation, and imagination. The self is not a development, except by the usual fiction of history, but a slow explosion, like that of trees into the sky.

8. Something about the starling in the top branches of the maple tree outside the window — whistles up — short-winded — light-fingered — half-baked — melodic wise-cracks. It's mimicking, even mocking, the melodies of the other birds now long gone south — those "chic transients". Another STARLING POEM! Can't get enough of them. Merlin says they must be my totem. Yesterday on campus, they filled every branch of a bare poplar in the middle of a field.

TWO

1. These mornings the sparrows set themselves out like blossoms on a bush, as if they had chosen their positions in imitation of the blossoms on the snowball bush. They move around on the branches in ones and twos, sometimes flitting to the feeder for a few minutes and then returning. A very domestic bird, I think, they look comfortable and homey, clustering around the tube-feeder, waiting for a perch, elbowing each other off, some of them in the sunflower seed dish (we have very small black sunflower seeds this year, which all the birds seem to like). We're still waiting for the juncos. The sparrows flare out like a fan and collapse on the bush again, waiting.

2. Therapist: Why do you suppose that neighbor was kind to you when you were a child?

   Self: Maybe because he was sorry for me?

   Therapist: Is it so hard to imagine that he *liked* you?

3. I haven't looked at them for several years, but I remember vividly some snapshots of my father taken when he was a young man, before he met my mother. They might have been taken on the same winter day, probably a Sunday, because he is wearing a tie and an overcoat and a snap-brim fedora. The pictures were in an album we inherited when my Grandmother died, in the fall of 1939. He looks very handsome, smiling as if to dare you to doubt his confidence in his good looks and his right to get what he can with them. Maybe he's just laughing at the photographer, who was probably his sister Clara.

In my memory the snapshots are very clear and sharp. It is a sunny day and the brim of his fedora half shades his face. His head is inclined a bit and turned so that he seems to be smiling up from under. He looks as if he was caught on his way somewhere and just paused long enough for my Aunt to snap off a couple of shots. He's probably about 16, and looks the way I remember my son looking at that age when he travelled with me in Mexico.

4. Impossible to avoid the idea of a *contract* for any writer. Ideally the text is open everywhere, a random collection of fragments inviting subversion or interpolation at any moment, never really condoning its obvious structure or development. But how to choke off intention or escape the conventions that will always determine succession, for example, or pre-empt a reader's claim to decipher meaning.

The question, of course, is why try to do this at all. What *good* is it? Why can't I get off the subject, as they say. The old question in this country: Who do you think you *are*. And Pearl's answer: Well, who *do* you think you are?

5. The year 1833 opened cold and stormy. The new fangled sulphur matches were proving a great boon, and the old methods of making fire were being fast replaced. There would be no more tinder boxes with their bits of bark, charred linen, or paper soaked in salt peter; no more skinned knuckles from fumbling with flint and steel while fingers were numbed with cold; no more trips to a neighbor's house on a frosty morning to borrow some fire. [*The History of the Town of Dundas*, Part One, 8]

6. "Naval aviation" — from a dream in which my computer broke down. This was the morning after watch-

ing a TV show on penguins: amazement, after their stiff-legged walk to the water and their clumsy tumble in, to see them under the surface flying, now as swift and elegant as angels should be. Pearl wanted to insist that the words meant something to me — why remember them otherwise: my own need to find the medium that lets me fly.

7. *self, ego; oneself, I*. I myself, me, myself, my humble self, number one [informal], yours truly [informal]; inner self, inner man; subliminal or subconscious self; superego, better self, ethical self; other self, alter ego, *alter, alterum* [both L].

8. Each morning I sit looking through a thick mesh of bare branches at a split scene: the upper half is pale blue at the top, coming down to a lighter blue, and then pinkish purplish at the bottom, which is the roof-line of the houses on the next street over. The lower half is almost uniformly dark, though there is a familiar rectangle of yellow light in one house. Some mornings there are two or three brighter lights, and often a woman and her small child move around downstairs in one house with the lights on, while the upstairs is still dark. All this becomes a kind of blank on which I project as I sit here, the meshing of the branches especially useful for meditation.

THREE

1. Coming home from school, a winter day in 1942 or 43, several big boys start to beat up a small boy, pushing him from behind, tripping him, twisting his arms. But unexpectedly he refuses to beg them to stop, instead lowers his head and flails with skinny arms. Knocked down over and over, blood and snot running from his nose, his breeches torn at the knee and filthy. He has scratched the lead bully across the cheek, a taboo for boys fighting. He fights like a girl. But he does not stay down, even when they hold him or put a foot on his stomach. Finally one says, He's crazy, leave him alone. But he won't let them leave him alone, runs after them, smashes them on the backs of their heads, kicks their legs. Until they all run off in different directions, laughing at his ineffectualness. His craziness. Ready to be killed for nothing. Nothing. After, even the other small boys are embarrassed by him, the insanity of his fighting. Even though he gains immunity from the small cruelties and tortures of smaller kids by bigger, nobody admires him. He remains a weakling to them. He is a sissy. Crazy. This is not me, but a neighbor boy named Jimmy whose mother asked me to look out for him on the way to school, to protect him. Naturally I betrayed him, and just as naturally he forgave me.

2. When I say I. Henry James writes in his autobiography of the fancy that he could reach back into the past to take the hand of the small boy he had been and lead him tenderly up to the present of the elderly man writing. But if I write myself, can I be said to be my writing. Do you read my I to learn how to recognize I or to read writing. A small boy at the kitchen table listens to the talk of adults in the garden while playing a game with his sister. Sometimes for hours in the writing of a poem I am nothing but the working out of the poem through all the impediments to artic-

ulation. I change, I delete, I recover, I redistribute, but 'I' do not exist, there is no *subject* anywhere here, only something unfolding by fits and starts, a way of saying but not the saying itself. You cannot identify this I and you cannot recover it from the text. It is not hidden inside or outside. There is no self-consciousness; only, if I am successful, language freed into play. It was always there, only accidentally connected to I. An I.

3. On March 1st, 1836, the contractor on the canal reported 2,500 yards excavated to a depth of 6.5 feet; 700 yards to 4.5 to 5 feet; 549 yards now in progress; 980 more yards to be dredged; 1988 yards in the creek, and now deep enough; making a total of 6,777 yards to Burling-ton Bay, with a water surface width of sixty-six feet. [*The History of the Town of Dundas*, Part Two, 22]

4 At this age, distracting symptoms of physical distress: intermittent ringing of the ears, almost certainly caused by food allergies; so-called "irritable bowel syndrome"; in 1972 some kind of prostate trouble caused by extended celibacy. [A prissy little doctor at Toronto General put my legs into stirrups, peered up my penis, advised me to resume regular sex. I was about to travel to Mexico, I said, where I didn't expect to find any partners. He looked down at me with distaste. "Masturbate," he said levelly and witheringly.] My poor back; the bone spurs (fasciitis); the aching right knee that has almost no meniscus; the recurring fungal infections between my toes and in my toenails; impotence. There is a man I meet only in the sauna at the Y who shares symptoms and prognostications with me almost weekly, oddly comforting for both of us, I think.

5. Early morning voices. Incessant, haranguing, belittling. My guilt, my shame, my dread. I cringe, curl into a ball under the covers, it is like a deep aching without physical pain, like the horror of migraine but spiritual rather than

physical. It took me a long time, years and years, to realize that I have always heard them, actual voices whose owners I sometimes recognize droning in disapproval, sometimes no more than repeating my name in every inflection of disappointment and contempt. They are permanent now, my lot, and maybe no different from what others experience. So — let them speak, but turn the volume down, Pearl says. Give them less authority without challenging their right to exist. In other words, acknowledge — and maybe this is just the appropriate time of day to do so. So — let me listen, and weigh, and analyze them textually (what model of discourse do they imitate?) and let me *use* them. All the remembered experiences, however sordid or shameful — however much thinking of them fills me with fear and bitterness and some seem so bad and so irredeemable that only death appears as any end to the damage suffered and caused — all of them can be written about. When I write them, I can shape them and subject them to language, soundbonding, punning, repetition. Let them have energy and authority, but not theirs alone.

6. **psyche, spirit**, spiritus, **soul**, *âme* [Fr.], **heart, mind**, anima, *anima humana* [L]; shade, shadow, manes; breath, pneuma, breath of life, divine breath; *atman, nephesh, buddhi, jiva, jivatma* [all Skt]; ba, khu [both Egypt. myth]; ruach, nephesh [both Heb]; spiritual being, inner man, "the Divinity that stirs within us" [Addison]; **ego**, the self, the I.

7. The family across the backyard is always up earlier than I am — before six, at least — and always keeps the light on after I have gone to bed, which is usually 11. The child is probably in bed earlier, but when do the parents sleep? They show no signs of listlessness in the mornings. Rather, they move around quickly and, it seems from here, efficiently. I'm not really obsessed by them. It's just that their window is the only visible human thing at this hour.

8. Starlings. They collect at dusk in the trees north of the Physical Sciences building, hundreds of them, maybe thousands, all singing short phrases and brief fragments of melody, growling and churring, as if going over their lessons or tuning up before a concert, but the concert doesn't come, *this* is the concert, post-modern music without closure, allusions to the inconceivable and unpresentable. They hop from branch to branch according to some system that keeps them roughly the same distance from each other, willingly giving up their perch when another wants it. [I remember Konrad Lorenz writing about flocks in *On Aggression*.] They sing their places in the trees — *I am here! I am here!* Shifting, flying off and back, settling in with little shivers of wings and tails, churring, bursting into short phrases. Then gradually the songs die down to small muted croaks, fainter and fainter, until there are only two or three, like children at the cottage, drowsily calling back and forth from their beds.

FOUR

1. From early days in childhood a fear that I did not exist, or not as others apparently did. I was like James's blinded seeker, watching others to try to learn how to behave. If I was successful in simulating their apparently automatic and unconscious actions, maybe I could *be* as at ease as they were. When I was alone it didn't matter, that is, it didn't bother me very much. When I was reading or writing I lost all sense of it. The danger, apparently, was in being detected as a fraud. I used to think, and eventually managed to say to Pearl during one of our early therapy sessions, that I was probably a Martian. It may have grown out of an early hope, then a conviction, that I was not really my parents' child — a thought that comes back now from reading R. D. Laing many years later, then Fritz Perls, then Jung, and only later Freud. But it was Laing who gave me (back) to myself, or at least gave me some strategies for distinguishing the operations of the false-self systems and exposed the rules for suppressing acknowledgement of them, and for suppressing acknowledgment of the rules themselves.

2. The farm horses pulled their wagons down Ogilvie Street, past the Mountain View Dairy, to King Street, and then swept around in an awkward noisy curve past Grafton's Department Store to come up outside George Laing's General Store, which every child on my street understood was a farmer's store, not a place where our mothers would want us to buy food. A very deep memory, I sometimes still dream it. The horses are huge and dangerous because of their heavy hooves and their habit of throwing their massive heads up and down unexpectedly. They could knock a small boy over by accident. But they are gentle, benign creatures, with sad eyes that seem to look out of their long faces with some knowledge of their imprison-

ment in this ungainly form. I know I was very small when that image was imprinted, because I am looking up and reaching high to touch their sloppy lips and wet noses.

3. Sometimes, writing at night, I would see — vaguely, I could never make out any features — a person moving back and forth across the lighted window of the house whose back faced me in the mornings. I thought it was a man, engaged in some kind of repetitive work, sorting something, maybe a manuscript. There are two or three writers in this neighborhood, one cartoonist for the daily paper, at least one artist (one of whose shows we attended in which he had wrapped bricks of wood in dozens of butter wrappers from small Ontario creameries). Then the light goes out and I see the figure emerge in a downstairs window, it is the man, and the woman joins him and they embrace. Lifting my spirits.

4. Drove into the country yesterday by myself, just like those Sundays fifteen years ago when I was living alone. North and east of the city on back roads:

> Bad roads and farms gone over
> to neighbors who rent them
> from the bank. The houses empty,
> tools still hanging in the sheds.

Something there maybe. My eyes feel refreshed by the long vistas. But there are too many small factories and service-malls and boarded up family restaurants, and, though I know I'm romanticizing, I feel sadness for the people living so poorly.

> Carcasses of trucks and cars bleach
> in the front yard, two generations
> of bad stomachs and weak eyes.

5. The year 1837 was an outstanding year for Dundas history. The big event was, of course, the official opening of Desjardins Canal, which brought a boom of prosperity to the town ... On April 18, Mr. D.C. Gunn sent two bateaux, each ninety feet long, and each carrying three hundred barrels of flour, down the partly completed canal and into Burling-ton Bay. Each batteau had a four man crew, who took only one day to pole the boat to Dundas, load it, pole it back to the bay, and unload it into a schooner in the bay. [*The History of the Town of Dundas,* Part Two]

6. Woke this morning at 5:15 from a dream, laughing. Something involving a class, some hilarity that had me borrowing a brightly colored shirt from a student, meeting two of my colleagues on a street, their amusement, and the student running up asking for his shirt back. I promise to return it, but don't by dream's end. Just on the verge of waking I remember the student's name: John L'Heureux, and laugh at the transparent ingenuity of my dream self. Wore it all day.

7. **self, ego, oneself, I**. myself, me myself, my humble self, number one [informal], yours truly [informal]; inner self, inner man, subliminal or subconscious self; superego, better self, ethical self; other self, alter ego, *alter, alterum* [both L.]

8. I always started to tell the truth when there was about five minutes left in my therapy sessions. Before that, nervous joking, verbal shrugging, "testifying", shedding selves like layers of clothing. I must have a hundred tapes of these sessions that I haven't listened to, probably won't, yet can't bring myself to tape over them with music or something else.

FIVE

1. When I was young there were still a few boathouses, weathered, almost falling down, on the banks of the Canal where old men (my grandfather was one of them) gathered to drink in the evening. We stole old rowboats and punts, some of whose owners it was said had been dead for years, and paddled with any pieces of wood we could scavenge down past the sandbar at the mouth of the Creek and into the marsh, Coote's Paradise. We fished for catfish, but our real targets were the enormous snapping turtles that slipped off the banks and followed the swirls our paddles made in the water. Sometimes they surfaced next to the boat and locked their jaws on the paddles, thrashing and pulling with impossible strength until we let them have the paddles. It was said they'd bite your pecker off. When we trapped one on land we tormented it with sticks and rocks, until it rushed at us hissing with hoarse fury. Dangerous and scary, it looked like nothing else in our world, spread-legged, glaring at us. Weary hatred.

2. The subject (in its identity with itself, or eventually in its consciousness of its identity with itself, its self-consciousness) is inscribed in language, is a "function" of language, becomes a speaking subject only by making its speech conform — even in so-called "creation", or in so-called "transgression" — to the system of the rules of language as a system of differences, or at very least by conforming to the general law of différence. [Jacques Derrida, "Différance"]

3. Therapies. The young psychiatrist with a dozen pipes in a rack on his desk, their bits all ruined by excessive biting. He looks stern: *How long have you had the fantasy that you are a writer?* "Doctor Solace" who took long phone calls

from his disturbed daughter during my sessions. He advised me to go to Las Vegas and gamble. The Thursday Group meetings: the woman who had beaten her little dog and whose last psychiatrist had fucked her, for therapeutic reasons; the man who could not stop thinking, the church worker who believed every man she met wanted to rape her; the baker who wanted to help her play out her fantasy, and his wife who left the darkened room never to return. The psychologist who wired me up and showed slides of ships passing through the Welland Canal, interspersed with nude boys and nude women with large breasts. *Why do you always make jokes,* he asked me.

4. Across the back yard, they have only the back lights on, so they are silhouettes. He seems to be fully dressed, with his coat on, she is in her night clothes. I think they are saying goodbye. They make one silhouette that breaks and reforms. I see no sign of the child. What's this? Are they dancing? Maybe it's not the man I'm used to seeing. Maybe he's away and this is her lover. Now they stand apart, then come together again. They are surely kissing this time. Fascinating. They are so far away I can only tell by the way they move which sex they are. I wish them well, it is a great pleasure for me to see all these signs of affection so early. There goes his car up the alley, he's on his way to work.

5. Starling poem: high in the maple — change in the weather — whistles up — light-headed — sends up — send-ups — the comical quality, he's a joker mocking the other birdsongs — fetching — his high spirits — risks — feats — grace notes — the other birdsongs are fat mouthfuls — he's so high he collects the sun — sun's leavings — old scores — short-winded — light-fingered — quips — sips — glint — scraps — snippets — thin air — windy — rasps — flippant

— hints — abandon — transients — picking up the left-
overs — Title and first line: This Winter Even Song? The
starling is not reconciled. To what? He is feeling bad-tem-
pered, regarded as a pest while the fashionable trendy
birds get all the attention. He's like the seals, disreputable
and nonchalant? I like chic transients for the absent birds,
in Arizona and Mexico for the winter.

6. In 1833, twenty-two-year-old
Bernard, or "Barney", Collins
arrived in Dundas from Ireland,
and started a saloon on the south
side of King Street, second lot
west of Ogilvie Street, in a
small wooden building that was
torn down about 1868. He suc-
ceeded so well that he was able
to build in 1841 his much larger
"Collins Hotel" across the road,
— a hostelry that still caters to
the public today, the oldest con-
tinuously operating hotel in
Ontario. Barney operated this
fine hotel until 1878, and died
two years later at the age of 68.
His son Frank J., nicknamed
"Bony", was proprietor from
1878 to 1913, then Fred Howe
until 1916, James Howe until
1929, Edgar J. Lowry until 1951,
and H. Gordon Smith until the
present (1966). *[The History of
Dundas,* Part One, *35]*

7. My father's mother lived with my aunt Clara in Toronto,
in an apartment on Jane Street near Bloor. I thought it was
funny to have a street named after a girl. She was sometimes disapproving (*You make those noises in the bathroom,
not in the parlor*) but she was also funny and her clothes
smelled of lavender. She let me read out of *Joe Miller's Joke
Book*: When is a door not a door? When it's ajar. Why is a
photograph like a family with the measles? Because one is
a sick family and the other is a facsimile. I was seven and
could read. I see now that she took children seriously, as
people. We walked and rode the streetcar to different
places in the neighborhood, to High Park, for example,
where we sat on a bench and watched men diving from a
high tower into the pool across Bloor Street. She talked to
me as if I might have opinions worth listening to, and she
argued with me seriously about them. Many years later I

learned that she had been a frontier cook in Manitoba and that after her husband's death [when my father was only 2] she supported the family for some years in the north of Hamilton with her cooking. When she died, on the same day War was declared in 1939, my sister and I were left with an aunt and not allowed to attend the funeral.

8. For the zoo poems, I need something about the condors. The seal poem is good, and the gorilla one, and the tortoise, and there's some stuff I can use about the ginkos and the bears. The condors sit high up on pieces of tree trunk in gigantic cages like parrots' cages, either motionless as if asleep and impervious to my kids' attempts to startle them by yelling or grooming themselves, spreading their wings as if to air them, opening the feathers at the tip like fingers. Jenny was thrilled when I pretended to swoop down on her and pick her up and swing her out and around, I was the condor. Jet black, the kind of black that is so matte it seems to contain a deep layer of slate gray within.

SIX

1. The town library was a Carnegie Library, one of thousands in towns across the continent. Where else could a boy of 13 in a small town in Ontario read Alexander Woollcott and Don Marquis and Dorothy Parker? Winter evenings I cruised the Adult stacks, reeking with overheated varnish and wax, looking for sophistication. I read _Out of the Night_ by Jan — ?, my introduction to Nazi terror. _Mathematics for the Millions_, for a few weeks I knew more than I would ever know again about the subject. Kenneth Robertson and the American Revolution and frontier, John Philip Marquand, Tolstoy, James Fenimore Cooper, Melville, Jack London, John Steinbeck, Hemingway. I flipped through the pages looking for dialogue, a good sign always. The air was dry and gritty, smelled of glue and brittle paper and the librarian's perfume and varnish varnish varnish.

2. Pink and pale violet above the roofs across the way on Rusholme Road, and catching some small violet clouds higher up the sky. To the south the violet is deep at the bottom, rising to pink, and then a kind of indeterminate shade of yellowish white below the light blue morning sky. All this changing moment by moment as I write.

3. Something about driving across the country, the sometimes obsessive _necessity_ to keep moving, some imperative that over-rides any consideration for scenery, food, pleasure. The mind is blown into the slipstream of trucks passing, an hour goes by without a single memory of anything, even of steering the car. _Where you come from is nobody's business_ . . .

4. 1835 Dundas Assessment Roll:
Total 104 heads of households + 297 other males + 313 females — 714 total.

Including the following:
Ansley, Samuel, grocer
Bamberger, Peter, innkeeper

Camp, Matthew, blacksmith
Coleman, James, (store, mill)
Johnson, James, barber
Leslie, John, (drugstore)
McDonald, Wm., innkeeper
Nash, Platt, hatmaker
Gray, Henry, brewer
Rider, George, tailor
Durand, James Sr., grocer
Gamble, John, innkeeper
Hackstaff, Geo. Printer

Paterson, John, brewer
Peters, Thomas, innkeeper
Reeve, Abner, saddler
Rolph, George,(gig,carriage)
Rourke, Thomas, blacksmith
Spencer, Joseph, miller
Weir and Spears, merchants
Witherspoon, Werden . . .
[*The History of the Town of Dundas*, Part Two]

5. Old age is best understood as a form of post-modern existence in which the mobilization of meaning is fluid and constant and confrontation with the self is continuous. So Haim Hazan, in *Old Age: Constructions and Deconstructions*, (p. 92). Again: In the cultural enclave constructed for the elderly, the old are stripped of their roles and symbolic trappings and excluded from the category of full human beings. Stigmatization and labeling ensure the imposition on them of a false homogeneity, and the humiliation and degradation they experience reinforce the analogy with initiates in a rite of passage, but without a socially defined destination for this transformative process (81). Or again: The central problem confronted by elderly persons is that they exist in a world of disordered time, a world in which time is fragmented, anomic, and unruly, as distinct from the time-world of the un-elderly with their symbolic models of order and harmony, and particularly of *expectation*, and *control*.

Living this way requires a great deal of determination and energy. The outer self may continue to act and interact in the linear, culturally acceptable manner expected and rewarded by the social environment, but the inner self functions differently. Symbolic structures create an atemporal universe of meaning consisting of significant memories, tokens of cherished identity, and freely constructed life materials.

This mental edifice is capable of accommodating infinite plausible self-images whose very existence serves as their justification. Like a nomad, the inner self travels incessantly without predictable destinations, never stopping long, never unwilling to linger, never pressed to arrive.

6. On the fairgrounds at Acton, one of the small carriage horses died on the track, just after its competition, while it was standing with the others, waiting to be led off. Without any warning, it tried to sit, to let its haunches down, but the shafts of the buggy held it up so that it merely sagged to the right. Its eye rolled up and it gave three or four grunts deep in its chest, as if it were trying to cough something up, and then it collapsed. Momentarily it hung in its harness and then it fell against the right shaft, its hooves sliding away on the asphalt track until it was almost lying on its side. It reeked of sweat and piss. The buggy teetered, half rising off the left wheels, but did not fall.

7. **Grade 4/Room 10/D.P.S. 1941** — chalked neatly on a small slate held by a sweet little girl in the middle of the third row of four, 33 children, 17 boys in the back and front rows, 16 girls in the middle rows. The teacher is not in the picture. I don't remember her name, or the name of the girl holding the slate. Most of the others I remember still as children: Cecil Goodbrand and Jim Lewis towering over the boys in the back row because already they have been held back once or twice and will end up with other giants in Grade 6, spread across the back of the classroom waiting for their 14th birthdays when they can get out and get a job. I stand beside Jim Lewis, called 'Baggy', half a head shorter though I am very tall for my age, which was 9 when the picture was taken. I am wearing a T-shirt with broad stripes and smiling broadly (one of only 9 children who could be said to be smiling; the others look alert and pleasant, some apprehensive, some bored, others merely

caught before they were ready). Nevertheless, my smile makes me look very confident. I have had many pictures taken of me already by my aunt Clara and know how I am supposed to look. Nowadays I like none of the photographs taken of me. I am the youngest in the class, having started school almost four months before my 5th birthday. I am in love with Beverley, in the second row four girls away, who has long blonde hair and an impudent beautiful face.

8. Some strange bird-cry, first like a rusty clothesline and now like a thin entreaty, repeating two notes, same rhythm, same intonation, over and over. It's our ignorance that leads us to make metaphors.

SEVEN

1. Barthes writes of what he calls the *diary disease*: "an insoluble doubt as to the value of what one writes in it." "I note with discouragement the artifice of 'sincerity', the artistic mediocrity of the 'spontaneous'; worse still: I am disgusted and irritated to find a 'pose' I certainly hadn't intended: in a journal situation, and precisely because it doesn't 'work' — doesn't get transformed by the action of work —*I* is a *poseur*: a matter of effect, not of intenton, the whole difficulty of literature is here . . . At bottom, all these failures and weaknesses designate quite clearly a certain defect of the subject. This defect is existential. What the Journal posits is not the tragic question, the Madman's question 'Who am I?', but the comic question, the Bewildered Man's question: 'Am I?' A comic — a comedian, that's what the Journal-keeper is. ("Deliberation" (*Partisan Review*, 1980). And yet.

2. At Eastend, Saskatchewan, prowling the town graveyard high on a hill taking photographs while Merlin sketched. Two of the long concrete grave-covers have broken and collapsed into the hollow holes — like bad plumbing in an old house: all that under the earth, unsuspected. Small animal tracks lead in and out of the holes. The bodies of gophers line the paths like dried leather flaps, victims of strychnine baits. Across the valley the north hills bulge like large bodies curled up on their sides under light summer quilts sleeping deeply while the placid cattle of their dreams move across them slowly munching the grasses under the power lines and up over into the trees.

3. The students in my Poetry Workshop conspire to arrive one day this spring with poems that all contained, buried in the lines, the words *dawn* and *summer* and *haze*. I love this whole question of Signatures, think of John Cage's

mad collection of passages from the *Cantos* in which the letters of Ezra Pound's name appeared without any of them being repeated before the full name was completed, so that the text became a secret self-identification over and over. It's true I never come on *summer* or *haze* or *hay* without a little twitch of recognition. In adolescence a dozen comic? variations: *Winterstraw, Blé d'été, Brume d'été*; then when I was, briefly and comically, a French teacher reading *La Tour du Monde en 80 Jours*, the students called me *Phineas Fogg* and then just *Fogg*. The most ingenious and probably accurate, *Sombre Hues*, during the time of my first, undiagnosed, breakdown in my early twenties.

4.   This winter even song
       will not reconcile
       the starling
       high in the maple

       who collects the sun's
       cold leavings
       out of thin air

       Then what?

5. William McDonnell was an excellent example of a pioneer peddler. His ancestry is not known, but he was licensed as a foot peddler as early as 1823, and did not graduate to a one horse peddler until ten years later. Thereafter his rise in fortune was rapid. As a foot peddler, he plodded along the side roads and back concessions, stopping at every farmhouse, and bringing a welcome interlude into the drab isolation of the pioneers. William brought news of neighbors, and the outside world as he displayed the wonders of his pack. The settlers could always tell when he was coming because he draped himself with tin cups, dippers, and sauce pans, which jingled as he plodded along the dusty, rutted roads. The tin really was tin, not thinly plated, quickly rusting iron of the later years. His pockets were stuffed to their bulging limits with pencils,

thimbles, needles, buttons, thread, cheap jewellry, jet beads, and two or three small bibles and hymn books. His pack was filled with cloth, — cottons, woolens, calicoes, flannels, prints, velvets, and satins, and with curtains, laces, and tapes for edging. He had whalebone for corsets, and hoops and tapes for hoop skirts; mirrors, rosewater, lavender, and toys for the children such as dolls, noah's arks, balls, tops, and games. How their eyes widened and glistened as wonder after wonder was brought out of the pack. [*The History of the Town of Dundas, Part Two*, 47-48]

6. **psyche,** psychic apparatus, **personality, self; mind**; preconscious, foreconscious, coconscious; **subconscious, unconscious**, subconscious *or* unconscious mind, submerged mind, subliminal, subliminal self; **libido,** psychic *or* libidinal energy, motive force, vital impulse, ego-libido, object libido; **id**, primitive self, pleasure principle, life instinct, death instinct; **ego**, conscious self; **superego**, ethical self, conscience; ego ideal; ego-id conflict; anima, persona; collective unconscious, racial unconscious.

7. What I have to say is not available, that is accessible. Saying that is what I have to say. Like John Cage: *I have nothing to say and I am saying it and that is poetry.* The interesting — and amusing, but also rather desperate — thing is the compulsion to say something. Williams admonishing himself in *Paterson*: *What shall I say, for speak I must.* Or: *If you can't speak, at least sing.*

8. Briefly the eastern sky from this window was gorged with magenta and purple and orange-red, and then the clouds, first long thin striations, now just featureless gray. My family across the way is not up yet, though it is already 7 o'clock. Suddenly I realize how much I learned to depend on them through the long winter mornings — as if they were doing my living for me while I sat here, like a character in a James story. In a few weeks I'll be able to open the window and listen to the birds, which I heard first this morning about 5:30 calling sharply and repetitively in the darkness.

Eight

1. Howard Norton was a childhood hero. He was the old-
    est son of the farmer whose barn was at the end of my
    block on the last field of what had once been a fairly large
    farm gradually eaten up by the town's expansion.
    Howard was a friend of my father, and a champion
    swimmer who competed every summer in the Lake
    Ontario swim at the Canadian Exhibition in Toronto.
    Later he joined the Navy and stayed on after the War. He
    was very handsome and well-built, called "Snaz" by his
    friends, for Snazzy. When I was very small he let me fork
    hay down the chute to feed the two horses and he took
    me for rides on the high wooden seat of the farm wagon.
    I loved it for the heavy boards smoothed by generations
    of drivers and the precariousness, so high and nothing to
    hold onto. The horses were Belgians I was told and I
    loved to see them tossing their heads and the harness
    heaving and all the metal snaps and couplings ringing
    and clattering.

2. At my therapist's suggestion I recorded my sessions with
    her, sometimes spending a half hour before our meeting
    browsing the tape of a previous session — that strange
    reedy voice I had to accept as my own — and then start-
    ing with a reference to something said last week. When
    I ended my therapy it seemed like an enormous amount
    of unwanted stuff on the tapes I accumulated.
    Unwantable stuff. *Unwantable self.* It had achieved its
    purpose, no doubt, which may not have been anything
    more ambitious than to let me for an extended time
    believe and act on the belief that I had something neces-
    sary or important to say or write. A terrain of common-
    place memories. A useful writer's illusion. But the mate-
    rial that builds up this way is its own referent. The phys-
    ical and the mental and emotional activity involved in

recording it and revisiting it is like the activity of physical exercise that pulls blood into the sore muscles.

3. John Salter's *A Sport and a Pastime*, Cees Nooteboom's *A Song of Truth and Semblance*, William Maxwell's *So Long, See You Tomorrow*, Toni Morrison's *Jazz*, James's *The Sacred Fount*, Faulkner's *Absalom, Absalom!*, Ford's *The Good Soldier*, Paul Auster, Marguerite Duras, Miguel de Unamuno, others I can't remember now. I believe I have always loved fiction that plays with the illusion of narratorial truth, that speculates about unknowables, and dreams up plausible stories to fill the gaps, without any more defence than that they *are* plausible. And whose narrators or authors comment on their own fumbling and improvising, even, like Morrison, confessing to envy for her characters because they have a real life, while the author spies on them from her window or stays at her desk, making all the necessary false inferences and projections the genre requires. Something like that in self-writing where the necessity of fiction is primary, given the operations of memory. And truth is . . . what? A name for the pleasure of writing and reading, the habit of recognizing *ways* of saying things our lives hold in common that apparently we can't stop saying. Think of an *oral* history of psychotherapy.

4. Writing in my journal every morning was an activity I came to love and depend on. If my early-morning voices woke me with their denunciations and scorn I knew that at the very least I could record them and even answer them — answer them *by* recording them. Issues of the virtue of what I wrote or its value were irrelevant when I was writing. Writing was pleasure, not even stolen but simple entitlement. Holding the pen, positioning the little journal, entering the date and the time, looking through the branches of the maple tree, sipping

coffee, and putting down words one after the other that were nobody's business, maybe not even mine if I chose. It was all signifier, without signifieds. I could write anything, that was the grandest illusion. I know of course that what I wrote was also what Barthes calls the *image repertoire*, what has already been written because it shares the writing codes of my whole community. But I was not I, selfconscious. I did not expect anybody, even myself, to read any particular part of this text, it was all produced with a sense that it could be changed or even erased. I could tear a page out of a journal if I cared enough, though I thought that if I cared enough to do so there was probably reason to leave it in! I wrote as if there were no subject, in either sense, the I was folded into the text that emerged on the pages word by word in my execrable handwriting. Since what I was writing about was not determined by any intention — except to write about my life — it had no particular urgency. Urgency, intention, value seemed far distant from any boundaries of what I was doing. When I stopped, it was to go to the Y. I would start again the next day, or skip a day if I felt like it.

5. April Entry: Slept late by choice — still very sick — must be flu and not just a cold as I had thought. My nose runs (*and my feet smell!*) and my head and throat are sore. My arm muscles have the deep fatigue that is like sweet syrup, heavy and thick. I am writing this now not for the brain or the memory, but for the body that is used to writing first thing in the morning. Writing with the whole body seems not so fashionable now as was a while ago. I suppose it was a reaction to "intellectualism", which was so severely denounced. It often seemed (Bly, Wright) a kind of smarmy mysticism, sacramental droning system regarding the images of earth and nature, and some yearning to *be* earth etc. At its origin this kind of thing is

amazing — Roethke — but it can go bad like vomit easily. So . . . the body heavy, sagging, the fingertips smooth/slick, reducing all sensations to mere surface — the old bellows heaving, the legs turned to wood.

6. Want to write something like *So Long, See You Tomorror* or *Montana 1948*. About kids and the adult world they have to try to comprehend. The boy is 13, modeled on Billy Best (which would be a great name, but I mustn't use it), living in that run-down house by the tracks just at the edge of town. His father is having some kind of affair with a widow somewhere on Hatt Street (her husband has been killed in the war). All summer long the boy's grandmother (father's mother) is dying in the upstairs bedroom. His grandfather, of the other family, his mother's, at 75 has become randy, living alone at the Hotel, joining a nudist colony up near Puslinch. The father takes the widow to the beer parlour openly, his wife knows and seems to tolerate it — a puzzling kind of matter-of-factness. Then the mother is diagnosed with cancer, tells no one, commits suicide (poison?), and changes everyone's life. The suicide does not kill her immediately, but destroys her stomach and leaves her in hospital drugged, never more than half conscious but still the center of power to whom everyone now defers because of her decision. The boy knows the facts, but is too young to interpret them, does not understand why everyone refers to his mother's "accident". He is terrified that something will happen to him too, equally incomprehensible and unpredictable, and he is furious with her for deserting him, can't stand to visit her in the hospital. So, the house without her — give him a younger brother. The widow comes in to clean it up, but the younger brother breaks down? The period of the story is the time it takes the two women to die, almost at the same time. The father and the widow struggle with their guilt — and

the town's condemnation of them now — then recover somewhat when the cancer is revealed, but can't go back, can't stand their happiness and relief when she is suffering so badly. The boy does something? Some boy's act of spite has terrible consequences? Or almost does? Give him a dog.

7. Women poets writing penis poems, cute things, trying I guess to domesticate the giant. Advice in a sex manual (*The Joy of Sex*?), treat it as a third person in the bed. Somewhere I remember a painting of a bath scene with about twenty nude men arranged in such a way that not *one inch* of genital flesh was visible. It was like a marvelous comedy, making cock and balls the only subject, the missing center of the painting. Was it at the AGO last week? I've got to go back for another look. Then the Y every morning, every size and shape, unexpected modesties and modest pride. Solly's song: "Big Dick Day at the Y". The woman in the Kensington Market explaining horse radish to my wife, caressing the shaft as she spoke.

8. Laing says that the most common situation he encounters in families is when what *he* thinks is going on bears almost no resemblance to what anyone in the family experiences or thinks is happening, whether or not this coincides with common sense. He does not mean that he is seeing them from a distance, as I am seeing my family across the way.

NINE

1. **Anamnesis**. 1657. [Gr]   The recalling of things past; reminiscence. The doctrine of A., in Plato, according to which the soul had pre-existed in a purer state, and there gained its ideas 1876. Hence **Anamnestic**, a. recalling to mind; aiding the memory.

    Nostalgia. [mod. L] A form of melancholia caused by prolonged absence from one's country or home.

2. A large crow sits high in the maple tree cawing loudly, watching a black and white cat, about the same size, make its way up the lower trunk. Then the crow flies off, cawing, until it is out of earshot (curious word!). A sparrow on the end of a branch just outside my window, feasting on new seeds, dipping into a cluster of them and coming up with a mouthful, then tossing away the unwanted parts with a quick flick. Apparently a delicacy, the squirrels sometimes eat them too.

    Then some vestige of a censuring morning voice insinuates with a sneer: you are wasting your time on these nothings, why don't you write about some troubling human matters, à la Somebody? Waves of anxiety, self-accusation, misery wash through me. I told Pearl these kinds of observations were valuable, especially when they make a poem, just because they *are* so close to pointless: that is, it is very easy not to see these things. My aim: to record them cleanly and not make too much of them. Get in and get out.

3. Outside the swimming pool in Eastend I asked a group of 12-year-old boys to pose for a photograph, and talked to them about the town for a few minutes. A short thin man wearing a jacket and tie — in that heat! — appeared from the door of the change room and said, What's going on

here? One of the boys said brightly, The man just took
our picture, Sir. No, Woodward, the teacher said wearily,
that's not correct. The man did *not* take your picture.
The *camera* took your picture. Without once acknowledging my presence, he rounded up his charges and
herded them down the street.

4.   The starling again:
       and whistles up
       light-headed
       grace notes what? on the wind?
       anyway, he is mocking the other, absent, birds — last
       season's *chic* transients —
Another pun for nobody but me. My best undiscovered
one — my old dog's *faux pas*. So far only Merlin gets
them.

5. Edward Hopper says, Maybe I am not very human.
   What I wanted to do was paint sunlight on the side of a
   house. [In Goodrich] He goes on in this style to comment on his painting "Second-Story Sunlight", The picture is an attempt to paint sunlight as white, with almost
   no yellow pigment in the white. Any psychological idea
   will have to be supplied by the viewer. Yet I know of no
   viewer who is not touched by this man's sadness and
   loneliness.

6. It is related that James D. Hare
   asked George Rolph how he
   could collect for some killed
   sheep. George said, "Identify
   the dog." Said James, " It was
   your dog, pay me." And George
   paid, but he also submitted a bill
   for legal advice. [*The History of
   the Town of Dundas*, Part Three,
   p.45]

7. What Pearl and I were searching for was the origin of my
   conviction of worthlessness and futility: the knowledge
   that I had done (or was) something so bad that it could
   not be redeemed. Not merely misjudgment but the expo-

sure of some generic fault: *there is something wrong with me.* My parents recognized it and punished me for it. At times I have seen a look appear in someone's eye that signals a recognition of it, and a drop in respect, a kind of distaste really. With all this, frustration and anger and shame — then, of course, shame for feeling the shame. Anger at *having* to be angry.

8. What is told is always the telling.

TEN

1. On March 8, 1836, the WEEK-
LY POST reported that a doctor had been called in a con-
finement case. When compli-
cations arose, he called in
another doctor for a consulta-
tion. They differed in their
opinions, hard words were
used, and names were called
such as silly, stupid, dough
head, liar, scound-rel, and cow-
ard. Finally one doctor
demanded satisfaction in the
form of a duel. After some cor-
respendence, the challenge was
accepted, and the date was set.
On the appointed day, the doctors met with their seconds,
fired two shots at each other, stopped the duel. They
persuaded the doctors to with-
draw their objectionable words,
but there was no reconciliation.
The POST does not give the
doctors' names, but there were
only five doctors in Dundas
then, Dowding, Hamilton,
Mitchell, Park, and Smith,
therefore two of them must
have been the opponents in this,
the only duel that actually took
place in Dundas (although there
have been some boys' fights
that were pretty grim affairs).
[*The History of the Town of
Dundas*, Part Two, 22]

2. A few minutes ago, slipping into the studio to let the cat
out, I saw the new painting Merlin is working on — the
drawing waiting for the paint. Two horses with stars and
moons on their skins, reminding me of the two horses we
saw in Cypress Hills Park when we drove across the
range to Fort McMurry. The drawing is of a
dream/memory window cut into the actual studio window that looks into the garden. She looks out this familiar window and sees the magic horses in the wild pas-
ture, one of them (as at Woodbridge Fall Fair) covered
with stars and moons, all the unexpected joy of that
moment when we met those two horses coming toward
us out of the fog and rain as we wondered if we should
go back, the road was so slippery and rutted we were
afraid of a serious accident. They nickered and came
shyly right up to to the car, probably hoping to be fed, but
it was impossible not to believe that they were delighted

to see us. Horsey faces, regarding us with calm interest, their hides steaming in the rain. Satisfied, they moved easily and comfortably away to browse.

3. Barthes writes of the photograph as a new form of *hallucination*, image of something that is not there but has been there; at the same time, or *in* time, irrecoverable but undisputable. Three of my class photographs have survived: Grade 4, Grade 5, and Grade 10, and when I look at those familiar faces I swear I remember the Spring days they were taken, the holiday mood and the strange panoramic camera that turned in a slow arc to catch us all, tempting some of the boys to jump off the bench and run behind the last row to reappear at the other end — they were always caught, another picture always had to be taken by the officious photographer from Toronto (*R. H. Peters, 137th St.; 2nd door north of P.O., NEW TORONTO, ONT.*) By Grade 5 the class has swelled from 33 pupils to 41. Cec Goodbrand and Baggy Lewis have already disappeared into adult life, leaving me the tallest now; Beverley's coy smile has turned into a bleak stare (she and Caroline X are the only girls, of 18, who are not smiling obediantly); Billy Best has joined us, with his Huckleberry Finn haircut and smile. You can see which children have been told often that they are *goodlooking* and which have never given it a thought. I could guess what every one of them is thinking about. Except myself. I remember the sweater I am wearing, a favorite, but outside of compliance my face tells me nothing at all. I am *one of them*, that's all: Lawrence, Dicky, Billy, Donny, Bruce, Jim, Ralph, Cameron, Jack, Caroline, Beverley, Ruth, Yetta, Shirley, Nan, Ruth, Bob, Alvin, Nort.

4. Do I not know that, *in the field of the subject, there is no referent?* The fact (whether biographical or textual) is abolished in the signifier, because it immediately *coincides* with it . . . I myself am my own symbol, I am the story

which happens to me; freewheeling in language, I have nothing to compare myself to: and in this movement, the pronoun of the imaginary, "I," is *im-pertinent*; the symbolic becomes literally *immediate*: essential danger for the life of the subject: to write oneself may seem a pretentious idea; but it is also a simple idea: simple as the idea of suicide. [Roland Barthes, *Roland Barthes by Roland Barthes*, 56]

5 Pearl was rather severe and prescriptive yesterday — while I was very contentious and evasive. She wants me to set a "frame" for our sessions in which what is at stake is not just relief from immediate depression, anxiety, etc. but a fundamental revision — an individuation — for the next 20-30 years. This means releasing the unacknowledged materials and *parts* of the self that have already been *amputated*. Either to say goodbye to them, or to comfort and correct them, let them heal. She was strong on assuring me (or this elusive self) that nothing would be profaned or invaded: this is not to be a denunciation of any kind. Rather, an acceptance and empowerment. There has been a powerful loyalty to the hurt and diminished self that keeps the other active self from accepting success or adventure. Loyalty to class, loyalty to my father's imprinted prejudices, etc. My childish notions of masculinity, being told (and telling myself) that I was *too* sensitive, that I cried *too* much. What did I do with my experience in terms of constructing a male model that would always elude me, though I could, or thought I could, simulate it plausibly. Is it true, as it seems, that I was *always* afraid of being found out by others, my counterparts, to be inadequate, as my father apparently found me?

6. The traditional view of a mirror is that it reflects a self, that it produces a secondary, more or less faithful likeness, an imitation, a translation of an already constituted

original self. But Lacan posits that the mirror constructs the self, that the self as organized entity is actually an imitation of the cohesiveness of the mirror image. [Jane Gallop, in *Reading Lacan*, 38]

7. A couple of starlings nearby, a single *pheero*, then a crow in the distance, then sparrows, also a kind of *squeeze*, as if the starlings were rinsing out high notes, now 4 or 5 pigeons swoop down to the ground under the feeder — all this just after I noticed the red sky (actually yellow sliding into mauve) behind the CN Tower.

8. Would I be embarrassed to be detected by the family across the way? I'm not really spying, since I can only approximately tell who they are, wouldn't recognize any of them on the street. They've become a mild blessing. I can project a sense of normality onto their comings and goings past the windows. I feel like the angel in the movie *Wings of Desire* who envied humans their absorption in mundane trivia.

ELEVEN

1. The little poem about the sparrow drinking from the leaf in the rain: I need some other images of dreaminess — the cat under the neighbor's shed, the mother in the house opposite pausing at the door to gauge the need for rain-gear, the yellow-green pears slick on the tree (like small lamps?). Some extension of the bird's act of patience and self-care, and also my reading all this as *dreaming*.

2. Yesterday Merlin and I went to three bazaars with my mother, the Seniors' Lodge, the Anglican Church, and the Catholic Church. Wherever we go in this town somebody greets my mother affectionately and they catch up on each other's news, who's sick or dead. With many of them she can't remember names, but old Mrs. Griffin in the Lodge cried for pure happiness to see her, and her daughter Shirley wiped away her tears for her with a balled up kleenex.

3. Back to Pearl and our "frame". The theme is adequate and inadequate masculinity, its roots in childhoood and its continuance in late middle age. Consider: a kind of automatic response to forceful or egotistical males as if they were *older*, that is, had a natural authority to which I must defer. Never mind that they might actually be younger, inexperienced, ignorant, I feel I should defer. Then again, what does she mean when she says that we communicate on the level of our animas? The anima communicates (is there a point to putting this down, so full of error?) by intuition and obliqueness, in fragments and discontinuities — by metaphor, especially, or by metonymy, which may be what Pearl is getting at. She wanted a word for the kind of effect we have on each other of being able to build on the words the other has used, as if we were sharing a mind, or at least a vocabu-

lary, and could use each other to generate from it what neither of us could generate alone.

4. **Relevance**: In therapy, of course, relevance, or at least relatedness, is the hidden prize you search for like a child trying to follow the string to the stash of birthday presents. The *pounce* of the therapist on the emerging connection is like one of those moves in sport where the idle shortstop suddenly goes into action and executes a perfect double play with dazzling grace. But before that irrelevance has to be learned. To be able to move through memories and associations freely without censor or program (without shame or blame) and, hardest, without labelling the material *trivial, crucial, brilliant, promising*. The analogy is with writing poems, when I fill pages with bits and pieces as fast as I can, to get *access* to the poem whose presence I can feel, just out of sight, beyond my grasp. With the poem, however, I can sometimes enter that place or mode where the self disappears into the gradually emerging text until the thing is finished — or until I can do no more with it, whatever suspicion I might have that some part of it remains intractable. That's where the analogy ends, since with therapy there are no completed poems, only snippets of insight, like narrow apertures you strain to see something clearly through and often end up only making out a vague presence of light, without any recognizable lighted object. I suppose what I'm doing here is trying to simulate that jumpy fragmentary tumble of *things* in an attempt to find something in the seams between them, the *différence*, the edges between, where it's not one thing or the other that seem to be touching, but the touching itself.

5. One starling sits out on the end of a branch, facing the other way. He has puffed out his feathers so that he looks large and round sitting in the cold wind.

6. In the Spring of 1973 I was living alone on the ground
   floor of a renovated house in the west end of Toronto:
   kitchen, two rooms, back yard, and a 3-piece bathroom in
   the basement. The rest of the house was rented as separate rooms, including what had been the front parlor on
   the ground floor, separated from my space by a pair of
   locked sliding doors. After a week or so, I still hadn't met
   the couple behind those doors, but I had heard them
   drinking and fighting so often I knew I had to speak to
   them about the noise. One night, when the shouting and
   banging were really intolerable, I went into the hall and
   knocked on their door. A small skinny woman answered.
   Her frizzy blonde hair was a mess and she was trying to
   compose her blotched, emaciated face into sober calm,
   opening her eyes wide and innocent. I guessed she was
   in the early thirties of a hard life, but she looked attractive in a stringy way too. I explained that I was living on
   the other side of the door, and that the noise was really
   bothering me. I tried to speak as mildly as possible.
   Before she could respond, a man came up behind her, his
   head just above her shoulder, trying to push her arm
   away from where she held the door. Then he stepped
   back and glared at her, never shifting his eyes to
   acknowledge me. He was one of those men you often see
   on work crews, short and wiry and full of rage, the kind
   of man my father called a shrimp. And he was drunk,
   with raging red eyes. What the fuck does he want, the
   son of a bitch? he yelled at her. He just wants us to know
   we're making too much noise, she said in a soothing tone,
   turning her head but still blocking the door. Why that
   cocksucking son of a bitch who the fuck does he think he
   is by Jesus if you weren't holding me back I'd tear his
   fucking head off and shove it up his ass he better not fuck
   with me if he knows what's good for him. He grabbed at
   her arm and scrabbled a bit but not hard enough to dis-
   lodge it and she remained as calm as before and said with

exaggerated reasonableness, Well, maybe he doesn't *know* that, Ed. He doesn't realize. Well, all right then, but he better watch his fucking step, the man said, mollified. We're very sorry, Sir, she said to me, rolling her eyes a bit, we'll try to keep it down.

7. In April, 1848, the new council quickly got to work on the new town's problems. Their first by-law restrained dogs, and the second restrained swine from running at large. They then purchased a minute book, ink stands, and writing materials. Some sidewalks were repaired, and some new two-plank walks were built; then they passed a by-law to regulate the exhibition of circus-riders, caravans of wild animals, and other show-men. The next by-law regulated ale and beer houses, oyster houses, auctioneers, and keepers of billiard tables and nine pin alleys; then came a by-law to tax dog owners. [*The History of the Town of Dundas*, Part Three, p.31]

8.   *This winter even song*

       will not reconcile
       the starling
       high in the maple

       who collects the sun's
       cold leavings
       out of thin air

       and whistles up
       light-headed
       grace notes taking off

       to mock last season's
       chic transients
       and their fat mouthfuls.

That's that, then.

TWELVE

1. In *Roland Barthes par Roland Barthes* (1975) there are two postcard photos of Bayonne, circa 1925, when he was about 9. Of one, Barthes writes, "Coming home in the evening, a frequent tour along the Adour, the Allées Marines; tall trees, abandoned boats, unspecified strollers, boredom's drift: here floated the sexuality of public gardens, of parks."

Near the end of *The Sun Also Rises* (1926), Hemingway's sad hero, Jake Barnes, stops overnight at the Hotel Panier Fleuri in Bayonne before moving on to San Sebastian and his solitary attempt to recover from the demoralizing fiesta at Pamplona. Hemingway writes, "There was a fine beach there. There were wonderful trees along the promenade above the beach, and there were many children sent down with their nurses before the season opened. In the evening there would be band concerts under the trees across from the Café Marinas. I could sit in the Marinas and listen." (232)

Question: What shadowy connections are lurking? What selves do we deposit as we go? In 1955 I was a beer waiter at the Collins Hotel, built in 1841, a regular haunt of my parents and their friends through the 1930's and 40's.

2. When my Aunt Clara died, after many months in the hospital for terminal cases, she took in a deep shuddering breath, like a long gulp of some delicious needed drink, and then, as we waited, she did not let it out again. It was as if she had slipped into another rhythm not accessible to our perceptions. As if she had not *stopped*, but just turned her attention away for the moment. We continued to wait, and then my mother said, She's gone.

3. Worked again on my little "Riddle" poem last night, compiling five different versions. Strange to realize I have spent so many hours on it, trying to get it "right" when it is so small and slight, the sort of thing I think I'll just jot down for the hell of it, not the serious stuff I want to be working on. I've done a lot of these little things — "bravura" is the model — where the obvious and limited begs for more and more time. Maybe this is the way these little poems achieve bulk and substance — all of it in absentia: the presence of all the discarded versions is very strong. Curious: whether all these choices and substitutions are still operative in the text, though not apparent. Are we always reading a kind of family of poems that resemble each other without being quite identical? "It might have been different" is what every writer knows, which means it *is* different. Try this: the pleasurable disappointment of expectations you could not know you have until you encounter the text that incites both expectation and disappointment. Not disappointment, but the recognition Lyotard talks about, of "the fact that the unpresentable exists."

4. Have been thinking about a kind of schema of textual activities for my classes, which also applies here. Something like this: in the middle, the *text*, what is present on the page; behind it, what the author intended to say (intended, say, under erasure as falsely confident terms), or says now/then s/he intended to say; in front, what the author thinks s/he has said; above, earlier versions, either parts or the whole of the text, that is, unused or rejected text; near this, other possible versions, whether or not intended, including synonyms, antonyms, etc. as well as variant idioms or constructions; then, somewhere (and this needs to be 3 dimensional), the meaning/intention that can't be avoided no matter how the author tries, his/her *imago* (unconscious image

or cliché, "which preferentially orients the way in which the subject apprehends other people" [Jane Gallop, 61]) that is always (potentially) accessible; finally, again somewhere, the meaning/intention that can't be expressed or presented, again no matter how hard the author tries, whether simply beyond his/her range, or a taboo, or part of an automatic defensive *gap* that can never even be anticipated; add to all this, around it perhaps, the whole potential and actual language practice of which the author partakes. *Then, around that?* — the voice(s) of the Reader, with all their variables. And all these voices speaking simultaneously, louder or softer, at higher or lower frequencies, etc. — my best metaphor for this is the car radio late at night while driving cross country: dozens of stations coming in and going out, loud or soft, separate or together, jazz, talk shows, news, sermons, commercials, etc. And static. And silence — sometimes silence like deep winds through empty spaces.

Questions: Who speaks/writes? Who listens/reads? What does meaning *mean*? What is *happening*? If communication, and expression, and representation — at least those versions we take for granted — are too complex to identify fully, what do we *do* with the parts of them we must regard as "irrelevent" in order to understand each other? Irrelevent must be ~~irrelevent~~. We cruise, we play, we translate (kidnap) texts into other structures, other *media*.

5. My earliest memory is not really a memory but a black and white snapshot of a little boy about two standing in a back yard (part of a wood fence is visible in the background) holding a long narrow board which I recognize as the prop for my mother's clothesline. I have just killed one of my father's rabbits with the board though my

smile shows no indication of guilt. When the picure was taken we lived on Dundurn Street, in Hamilton. I do not remember killing the rabbit — or eating it, either, which I am told I did, for supper. I have heard the story so often of how I killed the rabbit that it is now a kind of remembering. I remember hearing the story and imagine remembering the killing.

6. When focusing a camera you turn the focusing ring so as to pass the point of confusion, then back, passing it again, though not far past, then forward, then back, each time narrowing the range, until the true point of confusion (I never got used to this term) is reached, and the photo can be taken. The same with the memory?

7. Toonsky the cat is walking with exaggerated care into the deep snow at the back of the garden, shaking each hind leg as he lifts it, hating the wet stuff. Then he collects himself and bounds high out of it and down, and high again, his tail flinging out sideways for balance. Then he slips through the fence and slides under the shed of our next-door neighbor, where he will sleep most of the day, deaf to all our whistles and calls, until hunger brings him ambling back, a house cat again.

8. During this decade [the 1840's] some of the earlier, pioneer type industries disappeared, but others took their place. There were three new agricultural implement factories, nine furniture factories, two foundries, two planing mills, three distilleries, two stone quarries, three brick yards, two tanneries, and a woollen mill started, as well as several smaller businesses making axes, barrels, combs (for textiles), gloves, glue, lasts, lime, malt, nails, pottery, shoe pegs, soap and candles, and whips. Twenty-eight shops and fifty-seven new stores hopefully offered their wares to the public, grocery stores being in the majority. [*The History of the Town of Dundas*, Part Three]

THIRTEEN

1. Cholera came to Dundas in 1832 spreading terror because of its mysterious origin, its rapid spread, its terrifying speed in killing, and its appallingly high fatality rate. Parents feared to fondle their children, and everyone shunned the dead, fearing even to bury them. Prayers and doctors were of no avail. If you got it, you died. Cholera came again several times in the next two decades, but never again with the great terror of this first visitation. [*The History of the Town of Dundas*, Part Two, p.6]

2. I was born less than two months after my mother's seventeenth birthday, a few months after my father's twenty-first. My head was covered with long black hair and I had jaundice. My head had a dent in it from the forceps. I was long and skinny and weighed under six pounds. My mother says she tried to hide me when the nurses brought me in to nurse. The other women in the ward had fat pink babies. I was always a lot of trouble, cried a lot, unlike my sister who was always so quiet and placid.

3. First encounters with the Therapist are always played as comedies, not in spite of the misery of the Client but because of it. The Client cannot help re-enacting the insights of M. Jourdain, the hero of *Le bourgeois gentilhomme* — "I'm speaking prose!" In other words, these dysfunctions and paralyses have *names* that the professionals know, and that the client can learn. They are not unique: profound relief, even exhilaration. They are *problems*, and to say *problem* is to expect to be saying *solution* soon. This problem, that solution. Oh, boy! And so the client works hard to describe his/her life in such a way as to fill out the new vocabulary and begins to distinguish between the *hard* problems, or the *important* problems, and the others, the ones that can be bumped into

the margin. It is all very simple: the Therapist *knows*, and
the Client will *learn*, and be able to go on with life.

Sometimes, in this way, the Client can develop into a
pretty good, meaning pretty plausible, replication of the
Therapist, replacing one set of habits with another. Then
all that's needed is that the Client go back into the World
as a good convert, never forgetting the new rules, never
mis-applying them, remaining tolerant as hell of the mis-
takes of the other people in his/her life (who are not
Clients, of course), until the next prat-fall.

It's better, however, when the discovery of this taxonomy
comes as a disappointment: What, I'm just like the text-
book examples? And then the sessions become a war,
first against the know-it-all Therapist and her supposed
bullying, and then against the stupid Self with its stub-
born obtuseness and its blind loyalty to familiar pain. *I
will not change!* The Client's war-cry is pressed into the
closest sustained scrutiny of anything s/he has ever said
or believed. What *I*? What *will*? Change *what*? And so
on. Tears, frustration, defiance, helpless laughter, resig-
nation, comedy. Not the Madman's "Who am I?" but
Barthes' Comedian's "Am I?", the possibility of invent-
ing and subverting, getting on with it. Nobody's business. Or, Not Nobody's business.

4.   the poor despised pigeons
        nevertheless, wheeling
        in a flock, seem almost
        reckless, full of rare joy

Funny little things, these bits of verse, full of rhyming or
sound-bonding:

p: **p**oor des**p**ised **p**igeons
ess: des**p**ised neverthe**less** reck**less**
ee: wh**ee**ling s**ee**m
k: flo**ck** re**ck**less
fl: **fl**ock **f**u**ll**
f-v: **f**lock ne**v**er
j: pi**ge**on **j**oy
r: poo**r** **r**eckless **r**a**r**e
l: whee**l**ing f**l**ock a**l**most reck**l**ess fu**ll**

I could even defend it this way, as worth writing: the language having its way, doing what it seems to like, repeating meaninglessly.

5. Everyday rhetorics reflect spheres of taken-for-granted
   knowledge about the world. That knowledge, symboli-
   cally expressed and interactively maintained, preserves
   social boundaries and cultural classifications.   The
   nomenclature of ageing is a device for introducing order
   into an inherently ambiguous human condition.
   Designed to make meaningful the meaningless and
   describe the indescribable, it uses codes of sequestration
   and separation to construct a wall around ageing. Thus,
   while facilitating communication by creating shared attitudes, it also serves to perpetuate misunderstanding. So
   Haim Hazan, in *Old Age: Constructions and
   Deconstructions*, p.13]

6. Reading through the journals I kept all those months,
   page after page of anxiety, mortification, terror. My task
   was not to flinch, but to give it all words, to pre-empt its
   unspeakableness, to make it a text. Everyone knows how
   obsession sharpens the symbolizing faculties, so that the
   awful truth is visible everywhere, in the most innocent
   contexts.   So the passages, repetitive, redundant, out-
   raged, heart-sick, mopish — a storm of small details I

can't keep track of, misplaced and duplicated and jammed — they are so excessive they are almost exuberant, at this distance, even comic, without losing their power to call up memoris of the old bewilderment and self-loathing, like some cartoonish genie. Are they true? At the time I know I wanted to write the "truth". Sincerity was the first principle, which meant writing "raw", trying to write quickly and without "thinking", letting it come, getting it down, moving on until, like crying, it came to a stop on its own. (Yes, it.) I was so sorry for myself. Making it text, however, removed "I" and "myself" as serious candidates for "sincerity" and made them mere elements of discourse, arbitrary and conjectural. It was not (entirely) "I" writing, not (exactly) "myself" written about. Writing is reading, after all, and the "I" who was reading as "I" was writing, and who later (as now) re-read (and re-wrote), had no more claim to authenticity. I read these passages with dread — Oh, God, it was all true, and it's *still* true! — but sometimes, struck by the sheer insistence of them, I can't suppress a smile — whoever he was he certainly was *writing*!

When I read others' accounts of depression — recently William Styron and John Bentley Mays — I have the same mixed response. We want so badly to *testify*, and our subject is so banal. As one of Pearl's exercises for me between therapy sessions, for some time I responded to people's casual stroking gesture of asking how I "was" by responding that I was "seriously depressed" and "in therapy". At least I could stop being so depressed *about* being depressed that I pretended to conceal it. Blurt it out and take the heat. Some people, of course, wanted to know why, some even demanding angrily (witheringly), "What have *you* got to be depressed about?" but an amazing majority of colleagues and acquaintances seized the opportunity to confess, often lowering their voices to solicit confidence, that they were depressed too and that depression was ruining their lives. One colleague said, What's the point of trying to do anything about bad thoughts if they're true? What if it's just the way you are? She told me that, anyway, she couldn't remember anything that happened in her life before the age of 12.

7. A clear day, still cold, but still now, windless. For a moment the sun caught the trees in an orangey light and then faded, and they were dark. After the heavy rains of a few days ago our back lawn has pooled up (there's a stream crossing our property underground), flooded and frozen, still shining as the light fades. Along the back edge the ice is brownish, like a ring on the bathtub after a day in the potato fields when I was a kid.

8. Faulkner said wonderingly but apparently admiringly, in a review of Hemingway, that he did not seem to know any words whose meaning had to be looked up in the dictionary. Or was it did not use any words etc.?

FOURTEEN

1. Pearl asked, made me ask, of all my depression formulas and strategies: what possible benefit do they serve? In other words, though they may seem regressive, even suicidal, I must assume that my "Guardian Self" is trying to protect my invalid or immature self — maybe by simply removing it from competition, that is from the panic and expected pain of failing. Then the motives must be examined for reasonableness and present appropriateness: say the panic is a kind of blown-up and distorted kind of stage-fright, far in excess of what might be required to get the adrenalin flowing sufficiently. The feeling of self-worthlessness is a way of pre-empting criticism by taking away its *originating* power: so the Guardian can say, Oh, is that all? We've already taken that into consideration. So the outside world is never as hard or negative as the inside. Good luck.

2. My bedroom was at the front of the house, on the second floor. All night the lights from cars heading toward the City splashed up one wall and across the ceiling. My window was situated right over the sidewalk and I could hear every footstep on the cement for a long time, coming and going. Before the street was widened there was a huge chestnut tree on the grassy verge between the sidewalk and the road on the other side of the street, and at its base beside the curb a storm sewer intake backed up whenever there was a heavy rain and flooded the road.

   When my parents' friends, Bill and Elsie Friday, came over to play cribbage and drink beer, I always knew if they had had a good time because all four would stand under my window with last remarks and jokes for a long time, unwilling to call it a night. Then I'd hear the solid *thunk* of the car doors closing and still they would be calling out goodbyes and laughing for a few minutes more until the Fridays finally pulled away and I would hear my parents's voices, hushed a little now, going around the side of the house and in the door, and then whispering and rumbling and laughing downstairs inside the house as they got ready for bed.

I loved to kneel at my window and look out at the night street, especially in summer when I had a screen at the bottom and could hear the wind in the chestnut tree and watch neighbours strolling home from the hotels. Sometimes I fell asleep there, with my head on the cool sill, and woke in the deep stillness of the middle of the night, filled with happiness.

3. When I visited the Maya Ruins in the Yucatan for the first time in 1972, particularly the city of Uxmal, I felt their *absence* so powerfully I was embarrassed. I was a tourist, after all, staying at a tourist hotel just outside the site with other tourists — other Canadians, Americans, Germans — and I had no claim to any special knowledge or responsiveness, quite the opposite. Yet when I climbed the Great Pyramid or approached the Governor's Palace their monumental splendor did not move me as much as the realization that several of the huge hills around and between the monuments, covered in scrub trees and other vegetation, were themselves monuments that had not yet been excavated. I prowled the site for two days, in a kind of euphoria I had never experienced except after smoking marijuana. Wherever I walked, or sat, I felt I inhabited a zone of Unknowing so profound I seemed inessential, accidental, nothing but an arbitrary speck of minutia that might or might not have been there, might or might not have been the same person who boarded a plane in Toronto carrying the baggage of forty years of life. The ruins *said* a great many

things — they made the official guidebooks seem like absurdist parodies: I remember the glee with which we stumbled on a pile of ten or a dozen stone penises, five feet in length and at least one-and-a—half feet around, apparently removed to the dark shade of a grove of trees from wherever they had once been found thrusting out of the earth like the huge shaft (*sans* glans) before the Governor's Palace, and huddled untidily here off the main paths,

But it was what the ruins did not say, like an impenetrable text, that moved me, flaunting their showy surfaces like masks. What they did not say, what they excluded, hid, concealed, was what (I knew) made them intelligible — and that could not be retrieved, or excavated. And even if it could, that too would only be intelligible in terms of what *it* did not say . . . and on without end. The place was saturated with the vitality of its acceptance of not meaning. Which I, for those moments anyway, assented to unconditionally. When I returned two or three times in the next few years it was the same. And when my wife and I visited the Grasslands National Park in southern Saskatchewan twenty years later, that same relief from the assault of *meaning*.

4. The haiku is a very short form, but unlike the maxim, an equally short form, it is characterized by its matteness. It engenders no sense, but at the same time it is not non-sense. It's always the same problem: to keep meaning from taking hold, but without abandoning meaning, under the threat of falling into the worst meaning, non-meaning. [Barthes, *The Grain of the Voice*, 211]

5. Before I learned to write I pretended to know how. I used to take a piece of paper and a pencil-stub to a small passage between the kitchen and the hall, and cover the

paper with "writing", line after line of light scribbling and loops. Finished, I took it to my mother and showed her. I was writing, I said. Is that writing? What does it say? she asked. I'll read it to you, I said. And I read her the story of the dog who was bad and chased the chickens.

In Grade One every pupil had a small slate in a wooden frame and a slate-pencil to write on it. When we proved that we could write neatly without lines, copying what Miss Arthurs wrote on the blackboard, she drew lines on our slates with a wire contraption that held eight slate-pencils at once, and we learned to write neatly between the lines acccording to the Palmer Method.

I still love the look of neat handwriting, and I love the childish pretence that it says something and the loving con-spiracy of writer and reader that it says something shared.

6. As the ice retreated further and the climate became warmer, trees, forests, animals and final-ly men inhabited the land. The Indians who first lived in the Valley interfered little with nature except to hunt food and cut primitive trails through the forests. Today many of these winding trails are paved roads. York Road and Osler Drive continue to serve modern Can-adians as they served those in pre-historic times. The large number of these trails through the Dundas Valley was an important cross-roads even in Indian times. It was the eastern end of a portage which linked Lake Ontario to Lake Erie via the Grand River, to Lake St. Clair via the Thames and to Lake Huron via the Ausable. [*The Dundas Heritage*, I. D. Brown and A. W. Brink, (p.6)]

7. Now that all the trees are in leaf I can't see the family across the way except, sometimes, as a shaky light when the wind blows. I'm tempted, as always, to find some pretext to introduce myself to them. Hello, I've been watching you every morning for months as you get ready for work. I feel as if I know you. I know that they rise early, that they have a child, that they leave in a car,

presumably for work. At best, I saw them so indistinctly from this distance that I could never recognize them on the street. They're almost totally projection, a pleasant and attractive couple with a young child, living a quiet and regular life. I have not wanted to imagine anything more detailed or complicated for them. If they looked across to my window they would see nothing more than an outline of a figure sitting, hardly moving, probably reading or writing. A fellow early riser, another dreamer.

8. **European Starling** [*Sturnus vulgaris*] A gregarious, garrulous, short-tailed "blackbird" with a meadowlark shape. In flight, looks triangular; flies swiftly and directly, not rising and falling like most blackbirds. In spring iridescent; bill *yellow*. In winter *heavily speckled*; bill dark, changing to yellow in spring. **Voice**: A harsh *tseeeer*; a whistled *whooee*. Also clear whistles, clicks, bill-rattles, chuckles; sometimes mimics other birds. [*A Field Guide to the Birds East of the Rockies*, Roger Tory Peterson, p.256]

FIFTEEN

1. On our side of the street everybody had gardens, but on the
    other side the first half dozen houses — a row, all connect-
    ed — had small dirt backyards where nothing but weeds
    grew and it was convenient to throw unwanted articles.
    Cleaning up those yards meant collecting broken chairs
    and toys, pots with holes in the bottom, pieces of wood
    someone had once thought might be usable, and so on —
    and washing down the dirt with pails of water: very hard
    brown clay that was slick and shiny after such washings.

2. **Traveling**. The names of places, highways, the words for
    landscape, the local foods. assumptions about which ani-
    mals are beautiful, which pests. The Badlands with their
    chronic aloofness from human thoughtforms. Motels
    with their peculiar vanities and inexplicable oversights.
    The waitress had never heard of fresh fruit — she
    thought I meant had the can been opened yesterday or
    today. Driving across a perfectly flat section of Montana,
    watching a line of purple clouds race along a distant hill
    with, apparently, a road on its edge and cars with their
    lights on stopped, waiting. We all this time in bright sun,
    almost too hot to bear.

3. *Copy of the Statement of
    Losses Sustained by Peter
    Desjardins of flambora West,
    in consequence of the British
    force & the Indians being
    Brought to Dundas in the fall
    1813, after General Procters
    retreat and having keep there
    till their removal to the Grand
    River and the Westerd after the
    Peace:* [excerpts]

    — Six bushels potatoes took
    out my cellar by the Indians.
    — 9950 feet 3/4 in. boards for
    the upper floor of a two storey
    house 34 by 28 ft. & part of the
    boards were planed which the
    Indians took & made camp &
    destroyed them.
    — 294 parcels of fence rails
    burned by the Indians.

— Loss of the pasturing in my fields from the Fall of 1813 to May 1815. Four of the Indians' dancing camps was in the field & about 20 other camps round about & and they peeling the bark and destroying all my timber.

— Five hogs of about 1 1/2 years old, and one cow with calf killed and took away by the Indians.

— Jacob Cochenour swore that he saw the Indians dig potatoes in Desjardins' town lots; also that Desjardins had paid him $4 a day for hauling boards from the mountain in Flamborough West to Dundas.

— William Hare swore that he saw Indians take rails out of Desjardin's fence near his store house on the Big Creek at Dundas, and that he saw the Indians burn his rails in Desjardins' field in the fall of 1814, and that he reproved the Indians for so doing but they did continue their depradation.

(What a trying time it must have been for the women — trying to keep their homes intact until their men came back from the fighting fronts, and never knowing when an Indian might enter their home and expropriate anything that took his fancy. The Indians did not steal things, they thought it was quite alright to help themelves. Yes! It was indeed a trying time.) [*The History of the Town of Dundas*, Part Three, pp. 45-47]

4. —- **Syn. 1.** SOLITUDE, ISOLATION refer to a state of being or living along. SOLITUDE emphasizes the quality of being or feeling lonely and deserted: *to live in solitude*. ISOLATION may mean merely a detachment and separation from others: *in isolation because of having an infectious disease*.

5. Brought a little poem to my Senior Workshop, just to reassure the students that I was still writing as well as teaching:

Sendoff

I watched my life
with the usual interest

when what happened happened
my eyes were open

I've followed it now
almost to the end

trying not to blink
or let my gaze waver

I wanted at least
to bear honest witness

The students were civil as usual though anxious naturally to get on to the discussion of their own poems. But the
next day one of them, a young woman who had been in
an earlier class with me too, came to my office as a dele-
gate from the group.   After class, at the Pub, it had
occurred to them that the poem perhaps signalled my
intention to commit suicide. I was very surprised and
touched.

6. Psychotherapy must remain *an obstinate attempt of two*
   people to recover the wholeness of being human through the
   relationship between them. [R. D. Laing, *The Politics of*
   Experience, p.45] I love the precision of this: every word
   is operative and problematic. The *obstinate attempt* is *so*
   obstinate and persists over *so* long a time, with so many
   disappointments and premature celebrations; it is like
   saying that obstinacy is the paramount human quality,
   whatever the *wholeness of being human* might be imagined
   to entail.   Because an obstinate attempt to recover does
   not promise successful recovery, but only persistence in
   attempting. Etc. more on this?

7. Grayish blue sky with a long broad band of silver-white.
   A day that promises to be cold — wind-chill now makes
   2° equivalent to -9°. I'll get more wear out of my down
   coat which is such a pleasure to use. Yesterday I wrote
   myself into a good humor — reading and thinking about

Elizabeth Brewster's poems — particularly her persistent exercises on acquiring something new, a pair of glasses, a chair, or treating herself to lunch at the Faculty Club. Things *look* different, the old chair is still too dear to throw out, she is quite greedy all alone at her table. Then, some remark to a person long gone, her sister who was mean to her — *say it!* — a cousin she once envied. Sensible, self-respecting, perfectly calm and beautifully deceptively simple things. (The bottom of the sky is now taking on a mauve pink shade, very beautiful blending with the blue.) Earlier, around 6:30, the mother across the way was up before the others, walked around either naked or in something flesh-colored. She seemed to have several tasks that took her back and forth slowly and (perhaps) dreamily.

8. I remember only once when I seriously (or ~~seriously~~) considered suicide, driving at high speed on Mt. Pleasant Road just north of Bloor and almost turning the car into the concrete bridge supports. Lennie jumped from the roof of his apartment block, Brian into the Elora Gorge. His psychiatrist remarked to another patient, who passed it on as a joke, I don't know why he lives such a third-rate life. His best friend was married on the afternoon of the funeral. When news of Hemingway's suicide reached us in Winnipeg, where I was living alone and teaching Summer School, my first response was anger. I thought he had promised us to become an obstinate old man. I said a prayer for him at his house outside Havana 30 years later.

SIXTEEN

1. He writes Reviews and Introductions for the local newspaper's Book Pages that look as if they are intended for some future archival collection designating him as a Grand Old Man of Canadian Letters. For many years I have loved A—'s poems (yes, I can say love) and encouraged him to *work* the family materials, which promote his best writing. I first came across one of A—'s poems when I was a younger man living in X— and thought I might live there happily for ever, and I remember saying to myself, Now, there is a poem! Recently I returned to X— for a brief and somewhat sad renewal of my youthful memories — and was delighted to find that A— is still available in the bookstores I frequented, and still capable of producing those poems I found so magical so many years ago. And so on and so on. The result: a concentration on self so profound and unswerving that a reader is hard put to gather any information about A— himself. (Yes, I can say, bored.)

2. When my mother went to the Canal to skate she sometimes withheld the dime her mother gave her to use the changehouse that had a fire, said she lost it. Old Jack Auld said you girrlls, a Scotchman. A big joke. Age ten or so. Her mother gave her fifty cents to take to the House of Providence Picnic because all the other girls had fifty cents. A lot of money in those days, 1924. She won a prize of a twenty-pound bag of sugar, not the doll she wanted. All her friends took turns carrying it home, it was so heavy. Seventeen years older than me. We shared the same Public School teachers. Miss Arthurs. Miss Briggs.

3. Assumption: People write or relate their life histories to present particular images that they are interested in shar-

ing, promoting, and *working*. The same is true of the day-to-day recollections of old people as they apply techniques of modification and adjustment to enhance their chances of survival. The dearth of resources at their disposal compels them to use to the utmost all the means they can muster. Carefully constructed self-presentation to serve immediate ends is one such strategy ... Thus the haphazard, inconsistent, multidimensional events of a life are framed and organized to project a consistent, self-justifying story that makes sense and conveys meaning. [Haim Hazan, *Old Age: Constructions and Deconstructions*, pp.66-7]

4. A grackle sits on the TV cable wire in the wind. His top feathers are ruffled like a boy's jacket collar pulled up for warmth. His long spoon-shaped tail juts out rigidly, at a right angle, to keep him steady and balanced in the wind. All this in a second or two of confident perch and survey of the garden, before he drops straight down to the ground — and out of my angle of vision.

5. UNION CEMETARY. Located on Ancaster Street, this public cemetery was fenced at the beginning. It filled up in twenty years, necessitating the opening of Grove Cemetery in 1852. There were only a few interments after that, and, since there was no perpetual care fund, the Union Cemetary quickly became a weed infested eyesore that was not cleaned up until 1921, when Col. J. J. Grafton paid for the clean up, the collecting of the few remaining tombstones, and the erecting of them in the form of the cenotaph that exists today. [*The History of the Town of Dundas*, Part One, p.47]

6. I have long had a taste for discontinuous writing ... The implication from the point of view of an ideology or a counter-ideology of form is that the fragment breaks up what I would call the smooth finish, the composition, discourse constructed to give a final meaning to what one says, which is the general rule of all past rhetoric. In rela-

tion to the smooth finish of constructed discourse, the fragment is a spoilsport, discontinuous, establishing a kind of pulverization of sentences, images, thoughts, none of which "takes" definitively. [Roland Barthes, *Roland Barthes: The Grain of the Voice*, pp. 209-210]

7. In 1954 at Pickering College I held a special class for half a dozen adolescent boys with various kinds of difficulties in reading — nobody, I think, knew anything about dyslexia in those days. It was enjoyable for all of us mainly because, in my ignorance, all I asked them to do was read aloud from a few books I thought they'd like that wouldn't be on any of their other class requirements. They worked slowly through *A Streetcar Named Desire* and *In Our Time*, gaining confidence and some skill, and flattered by the *sophistication* of the subjects. Finally we reached *The Catcher in the Rye*, which I was sure would be a favorite, since so much of it reflected their own lives in boarding school; but to a boy they hated it, and hated Holden most of all. He did not have a good attitude toward his schoolmates (Ackley!), he was careless about losing the team's equipment, he swore too much, he lied, was disrespectful to adults, mishandled money, was stupid to wear his stupid hat everywhere, and so on. When I pointed out that he was in mourning for his dead brother, they refused to see that as an excuse for so much bad behavior. In the OTHER-SELF RATING QUESTIONAIRE the school administered in November and May they would definitely all put Holden in the LAST QUARTILE, among the failures and sociopaths.

8. **Subject**: A subject is a noun, or a noun substitute, about which something is stated or questioned. The subject usually comes before the predicate. The complete subject is the subject and all the words (modifiers, etc.) that belong to it. [*Writing Well*, Donald Hall, p. 450)

SEVENTEEN

1. **You could write a story about that.** Out to the Miracle Mart
   to buy coffee, stopped at the light at Dovercourt/College,
   saw a man cutting across the intersection in a jeans jacket and dirty white baseball cap holding on his upraised
   left palm a small model of a boat ready for painting. He
   saw me looking and veered over to my car and I rolled
   the window down. He was about 25, open handsome
   face. "Made it out of orange crates. No shit. No plans or
   anything. Just outa here," and he tapped his head, and
   we both looked at the model — complete to a small cot-
   ton sail — sitting on his hand. He was as surprised and
   impressed as I was. The light changed, he danced to the
   north side of College & waved. "Looks great!" I yelled as
   I drove past him. He had shoved his cap further back on
   his head and was holding his boat out to a young black
   woman at the streetcar stop.

2. Bad morning from 4:00 on. I am not good enough, don't
   measure up, fear scrutiny and judgment — being scold-
   ed! — and can't find any center or *first stage*. Too many
   demands, I can't do it, everything neglected so long.
   Spasms of excruciating shame and fear, futility, impotence — I want to rock and whine. I feel useless to
   myself, and as usual when this comes on I'm convinced I
   have cancer — in my armpits, moles, bowels, prostate —
   why not? When I was at university I often wished I had
   TB, the romantically disabling disease then, so that I
   could be exempted without shame or guilt. It would be
   fine, I thought, not to have anything expected of me but
   just to be allowed to be, and to heal gradually: my whole
   job just to take care of myself, coddle myself, and have
   others to do that too. I wanted to be taken care of, be
   loved for no reason, not have to earn anything. But none
   of my little break-downs were shut-downs. I believed I

could be cheerful under the most crushing depression because there was nothing else to be, others depended on me — and the terror of knowing I was simply inadequate, and that nobody else seemed to notice. Pearl says, You have to comfort that child yourself. He's very small and exposed. Suppose you told him, Look, I survived, it's actually not as bad as you thought it would be.

3. The way in which Canada's Native peoples have been portrayed in the photographic images of Brant County has been to essentially edit them from the history of the community's images. The images of the Native community have existed as subtext. Although the 1800's produced iconic images of Indians in their naive dress, the linear development of their community, the shape and form of their lives, the images of their reality, have remained separate from an integrated image of "community". In this way, the photographic image both reflects reality — the editing of the Native voice in Canadian society — and shapes society — the perpetuation of images of Indians as subtext rather than text. It is my final hope for the exhibition that the text is culturally shared. [Sharon Davidson, *Message Without a Code: A Photographic Exhibition*, p.19]

4. Before we went to Sea Cadet camp in the mid-1940's we had to submit to a physical examination. We were ushered in, in groups of ten, into the Doctor's examining room where we stood in a line, freshly washed, nervous and jokey. First the Doctor came down the line with his stethoscope and listened to our hearts as we held our shirts up to our chins. Then he looked into our ears with an instrument that was cold and hurt a bit. Then it was time for the short-arm inspection. We dropped our shorts and waited in a state of panic as the Doctor cupped two fingers under each boy's testicles (his bag we called it) and ordered him to cough. Invariably three or four boys got an erection as they waited for him, and his Nurse, a stocky middle-aged woman, stepped up and

swatted each boner briskly but not unkindly (*Down, wanton!*). That was Doctor Bates. Every year somebody recited: Doctor Bates! And his son, Master Bates! At camp Jim Warren not only ignited his farts with matches but hung two towels on his dick before it lost its 45° angle.

5. *Parents feared to fondle their children.* In my neighborhood if there was fondling of children it took place in private and must have involved a kind of guilty self-indulgence. It was terrible for a boy to get the reputation of being a sissy, and even girls were treated a bit coolly, at least by present standards. Of course, there was generally more formality between people in those days, and the famous Southern Ontario disapproval of showiness, even among the working class, with their standards of decency and decorum. I don't remember seeing *any* displays of affection in the families in our neighborhood, and it was something I had an eye out for, probably because sentimental affection was portrayed so often in the movies we saw at the Bijou Theatre. However, I remind myself, all this could change completely when parents, usually fathers, had been drinking, and smothered their kids with rough kisses and hugs and squeezes and maudlin babytalk. But nobody took that seriously, least of all the mothers, who were apt to mock them for such mealymouthedness; or the children who knew the other side of that rush of feelings. On the other hand, I can't entirely trust my memory on this subject.

6. From the window this morning I see, about 50 metres away across the backyards, a shaft of sunlight between two buildings on College Street and a swarm of flies darting in and out, looking very big because of the brightness they collect. They fly like dragonflies, hovering and darting, as if they were attacking each other. Oddly, they stay in the same spot just above the porch of the elderly brother and sister whose garden abuts ours

one of the sights of heaven
golden dragonflies
caught in this early morning
shaft of sunlight over my
backyard neighbor's house
hovering and darting as if
gathering light about themselves
to magnify their bodies
were their only occupation
and mine at my desk to witness
and record these presences

Something there, maybe.

7. There is no place without language: one cannot contrast language, what is verbal (and even verbose) with some pure and dignified space which would be the space of reality and truth, a space outside language. Everything is language, or more precisely, language is everywhere. It permeates the whole of reality: there is nothing real without language. Any attitude that consists in hiding from language behind nonlanguage or a supposedly neutral or insignificant language is an attitude of bad faith. The only possible subversion in language is to displace things. Bourgeois culture is within us: in our syntax, in the way we speak, perhaps even in a part of our pleasure. We cannot move into nondiscourse because it doesn't exist. Even the most terrorist, the most extremist attitudes can be rapidly recuperated by bourgeois culture. The only combat that is open to us is not frank, out in the open, but most often muffled, insidious. This combat doesn't always end in triumph, but it must attempt to displace, to shift languages. We are trying to create, with bourgeois language — its rhetorical figures, its syntax, its word values — a new typology of language, a new space where the subject of writing and the subject of reading do

not have exactly the same space. This is what moderni-
ty is working on. [Roland Barthes, *Roland Barthes: The
Grain of the Voice*, 162]

8. **Modesty.—N.** modesty; humility &c.; diffidence, timidity; retiring disposition, unobtrusiveness, bashfulness &c.; reserve, con-
straint; demureness &c.; shame, disgrace; humiliation, mortification; confusion; abasement, self-abasement: **self-knowledge**.

EIGHTEEN

1. For a few years on week-ends when I couldn't see my children I drove out of the city to take photographs in the countryside around Southern Ontario. I scouted side roads and back concessions, stopping at every abandoned farm house to record the evidence, bringing my unhappiness into the drab isolation of these places where something had gone wrong, where families had broken up and drifted away, leaving tools to rot in sheds and roofs to sag into upper bedrooms. Sometimes the houses had been used by lovers: a filthy mattress would half fill a kitchen floor, warmed by dead fires of chair legs and window frames, and a few bottles and cans tossed into a corner. The windows were smashed or stolen, half the stair treads were gone, six layers of wallpaper in the parlor buckled and sagged with mildew.

   But sometimes a rag of curtain billowing in the empty sash was caught in the sun, or snow piled in the front yard and on the roofs to make a curious structure of triangles like a Hopper painting, or a panel truck rested in an overgrown lane, tires flat, paint bleached in uneven streaks, pointed out to the road. They were exercises in composition and exposure to be worked out in long darkoom sessions through the night when I got home. I could prowl for hours along the dusty, rutted roads, ignoring the big prosperous farms with their mile-long furrows, in search of absences like these where the life had been reduced to a long dying down, and ghosts sneaked back like orphaned dogs to the long gone family energy they could just faintly remember. I took rolls and rolls of Tri-X film to develop, print into contact sheets, file in binders, and then mine for enlargements that might, if I was lucky, fix that sad time in an image that could thrill me. That had never been seen until I made it.

2. When I was a small child I helped my grandfather dig his garden with a child's size spade and put in chunks of potato and melon seeds and carrot seeds and beans and covered them up, and I watered the roots of the straggly tomato plants and watched them straighten and spread their leaves. I sat with him on the back stoop while he taught Nipper, his toy terrier, to perform tricks. Nipper could sit up and beg and roll over, and he could jump through my grandfather's arms when he held them out like a hoop in front of him. The little dog loved him insanely and was desperate to please him, writhing and wriggling with ecstasy, and then stepping off to the end of his rope and crowing like a rooster. My grandfather pretended to cuff him with his big rough hand and rubbed his skull with his knuckles.

   Sitting on the stoop I pressed against my grandfather's sour-smelling jacket while I listened to his long rants against my mother and grandmother. He could throw his voice up and down the scale like a singer while they stayed out of sight behind the kitchen window screen. I was thrilled by his bravura and like Nipper I felt deeply his grievances: how *unfair* everybody was to him, how *nobody* loved him but a dog and a little boy who didn't know no better. *Aaahaaaooow!* he would moan in his rough Cockney voice, *Naaahaaaoowboddy luuvs me! Naaahaaaoowboddy luuvs aaould Joe!* And I would say, I love you, Grampa! to complete the formula. In the kitchen I could hear my mother's chuckle and sometimes my grandmother's short bark of a laugh, tickled in spite of herself.

3. For the writerly reader plays the texts she reads, follows the signifying chains, the paths out of the text, makes substitutions and combinations only to see the more that can be made. To express a text is to take its signs out of their familiar contexts, contextualize them anew, and

recontextualize them yet again along the line sighted from the first new context. [Wiseman, *The Ecstasies of Roland Barthes*, p.175]

4. From earliest times, an Indian Trail existed from the Niagara River to Binkley's Hollow, and thence to Dundas where it branched three ways, one branch leading through Ancaster to Windsor and Sarnia, one branch through Galt to the Bruce Peninsula, and the third via the York Road and Waterdown to Toronto. Through Hamilton, present day Main Street follows this trail to Binkley's Hollow, and it is joined in Westdale by a trail that started at Burlington Bay below Dundurn Castle and followed Dundurn Street to the main trail. Between Binkley's Hollow and Dundas, this heavily travelled trail has followed at least three routes, called by Dundasonians, Peer's Road, Thorpe's Road, and The Dundas and Binkley Hills Road. [*The History of the Town of Dundas*, Part Three, p.71]

5. Just now, the sharp repeated cry of a bird I don't recognize and can't see through the leaves, followed by some obvious muttering and chaffing by two or three also hidden birds, these almost surely starlings. I seem to care overmuch for this life of the backyards that goes on and is itself whether we notice or not. *Feeo Fweeeeo* — they call at intervals as if trying out the sounds: starlings almost certainly. Someone on the CBC recently remarked that most people do not (*can* not) *see* starlings because of the bad reputation the bird has been given. Like the beautiful little sparrow it must be said to be ugly or drab, boring — since the ideology is that exotic-looking birds are *good*, the others *bad*. *Twee-Twoh, Fee-Foh*, isolated, then repeated, the starling announcement of presence. Better dust off those starling poems I never finished. The trouble is, I haven't worked out any *need* to say ___. Is it that they are content to disguise themselves, suppress the gorgeous blues and greens of their necks and heads, the spotting of their rumps and tails, and their intellectual

brilliance among the other bird-brains? That is, is the poem about the fact that they are *really* exotic and exciting? Don't think so. Better that they be *there*, accurate, for the few people (apparently) who know them than that I seem to be pimping on their behalf (and my own as a very sensitive person). Just the fact of them makes me feel healthier.

6. Yesterday my session with Pearl was delayed while she searched for an office we could meet in. I can't figure out her status in the clinic — a labyrinth of rooms of all sizes and shapes for examinations, X-rays, consultations, technicians, and whatnot, with three large and rather luxurious "Offices" on the outside wall. Usually we meet in a pitifully small inner room on a narrow hall where I often have to squeeze through crowds of half-dressed people clutching immigration papers on their way to the U.S. Inside, I sit on a low uncomfortable chair beside Pearl's desk facing the wall 8 feet away on which a couple of very crude small paintings are hung. I can hear the crowd outside and assume that they can hear me. But sometimes, like yesterday, this room is not available for some reason, and we end up in one of the big offices and try to accomodate ourselves to a foreign space. I felt a bit cranky at being shunted around and thought Pearl lacked respect — and so I did too. It was like an enactment of the situation that brought me to her — feeling out of place, not *authentic*. Stupidly, I didn't mention this to her, out of — what? consideration for her feelings? — and so I was feeling resentful and unresponsive, and blocked. She was unremittingly cheerful and bright — exaggeratedly — and I didn't feel as willing as usual to go along with her strategy of barefaced manipulation of my remarks. Later, in the car, I had to laugh. After all I had read about transference!

7. **Memorize**, v. 1591, [f. MEMORY + IZE.] **1.** *trans.* To cause to be remembered, make memorable; also, to preserve the memory of in writing, record. Now *rare*, 1591. **2.** To commit to memory 1856. A Cenotaph to memorize our grave 1822.

8.   riddle

the world
we see
through

the world
we see
through

NINETEEN

1. 8:32 A.M. An excellent sleep-in, with some good dreams: wandering through some informal convention hall, people in small groups chatting and drinking, all ages and forms of dress. I ask everyone I meet if they know where Bronwyn is. No-one does, but they are very polite and pleasant, some suggesting that I wait with them in case she comes by, but I keep wandering, no urgency, feeling relaxed and happy. Merlin suggests that I'm looking for Brown One, in other words a 'Nish, an Indian — Herself. *Of Course!* Strange to be sitting here with the backyards perfectly visible, after having watched dawn come so many times. It's a cloudy day, the light absolutely flat and even, good for clarity in black and white photographs. I must have dreamed of our old dog Deor, dead now two months — she's on my mind, her gentle loving gaze, and the unexpected thump of her tail as she thinks of Merl or me and how much she loves us. Angel.

2. By the time the news of the declaration of war on June 18, 1812 reached the valley, the settlers had already been alerted, but they received the news with a sense of unreality, a feeling that persisted until the first supply of government muskets and uniforms arrived. On August 8th there was still greater excitement when General Brock marched through the valley, and out the Governor's Road with forty regulars and 260 militia men, including some Ancaster and West Flamborough men in Captain Samuel Hatt's company. After picking up sixty Indians at the Mohawk Village, and other reinforcements further on, they proceeded to Detroit, where they not only captured the fort, but also the American General Hull's army of 2,500 men and 37 guns. The surrender took place August 16, only eight days after Brock had marched through Dundas Valley. Including all his reinforcements, Brock's force did not exceed 1,450 men and five guns.

In 1813, several wounded men were brought to the homes in Dundas Valley, and the flats at the west end of the community were used as a camping ground by Indian warriors acting as a flank guard for General Harvey's force on Burlington Heights . . . That summer, two thousand Indians camped on the flats, where they held a feast and war dance that lasted several days. They stole pigs, geese, chickens, and cattle, then feasted, war whooped, and thoroughly terrified the women who sent to General Vincent frantic appeals for aid. However, the children were fascinated; and, except for the lost live stock and foodstuffs, the Indians behaved very well. [*The History of the Town of Dundas, Part One*, pp.23-4]

3. Pearl suggested some close looks, from the viewpoint of the child, at important sexual episodes and transitions. Oh, well. A bunch of little kids playing doctor under the grape arbor next door, putting wide grass blades between the labia of little Neenie, who was visiting her grandparents there and initiated the game. The crazy old man who periodically escaped from his daughter's home and offered a nickel for a kiss, and once under the bridge at the Little Park at the corner showed several of us his thing, swollen and purple and alarming, and tried to get us to touch it. Two sisters — the "Logan girls" — from a *very* tough family — four or five years older than the group of boys they found playing in the woods by the railroad tracks — whipped up their dresses and showed us their "gashes", repeating remarks from the boys and men they had "done it with", laughing and smoking, mocking us for our ignorance. Their cunts had been chopped in them with axes, their cherries were pushed back so far they nearly choked on them, they got the curse and had to be on the rag. They made us show them, one by one, our little erect penises and (I think) touched some of them, saying things like, Oh boy, I wouldn't mind having that little pecker up my hole, and laughing raucously. I was terrified of them, but I wanted to *know*. They were very lean and strong, tough as boys

with careless stringy bodies, and pretty in a sharp-faced discontented way. They had a short abrupt way of speaking, scornful, as if they were always snarling or scoffing.

After that meeting in the woods I was always aware of them, living two streets over with a houseful of brothers, all of them lawless and brutish. I remember they were stars on the Ladies' Softball Team for one of the factories and played better than most boys, sliding into base with total disregard for skin-burns and cuts. I thought of them as very exciting, powerful, demanding, any man's equal in lewd speech and mockery. I think they represented a kind of fantasized freedom from the normal constraints of someone like me who desperately wanted to be respectable. They were completely out of that race, true members of the caste of the Town's poor: hard, brutal, coarse and uneducated men and women who fascinated me as a child. I didn't see them then as stupid or even reckless. I believed they were *choosing* their lives, as I believed I was choosing mine. No matter how successful I was (or hoped I was) in shedding my own lower class skins, I always secretly craved their approval. The last time I saw them, at least fifteen years after the meeting in the woods, they hadn't changed except to become older and tougher, frizzy-haired and sharp-faced, still playing softball, still mocking and discontented.

4. Evans' earliest photographs for the FSA apparently date from June, July and November of 1935, when he toured the coal-mining towns of West Virginia and the industrial towns of Pennsylvania. (The gap between July and November is curious, but there is nothing in the records to explain it). In what are assumed to be the first photographs, made in the Scott's Run area of West Virginia, Evans established the basic style for most of his FSA

work — careful, direct, detailed views of people and places, usually taken with the 8x10 camera, but sometimes supplemented by use of a 4x5 and more frequently a 35mm, particularly for studies of people. The Pennsylvania photographs which followed in July and November are similar to the West Virginia ones, with perhaps more emphasis on the man-made environment. The pictures in both series are characterized by a direct, almost formal confrontation of the subject with the camera and the photographer. [Jerald D. Maddox, "Introduction", *Walker Evans: Photographs for the Farm Security Administration, 1935-1938*, pp.ix-x]

5. At the hotel desk the young man who made up my bill had been reading as I approached. He laid his book down, a well-worn paperback that looked vaguely familiar, and greeted me cheerfully and deferentially. When I screwed my head around to read the title, I saw *How To Win Friends and Influence People*, by Norman Vincent Peale. Amazing. I had spent a summer with it in the middle of High School, underlining important passages, as advised, without any noticeable effect on either friends or people, though I remember being very earnest for a few weeks. What did he think of my claim to have read it 45 years ago? His skepticism was hard to smother, but he smiled anyway. Does it still apply? *Oh, yes! It still applies*, he said with a very confident nod.

6. It is fascinating to find that American Indian weather beliefs are similar in some instances to those brought from over the Atlantic by early European settlers . . . Here are some of the proverbs from various tribes:

A snowfall late in the spring, with the wind to the north, indicates that the snow spirit is returning to his abode in the north.

If chickens continue to scratch for food during a rain, it is an indication that the rain will continue for some time.

When the wind blows the leaves "inside out", it is a sign of approaching rain.

If the sun shines while it is snowing, the Devil is "pluck ing his geese." It will snow the following day. Dandelions blooming late in the season are a sign of an "open winter." [*Baer's Agricultural Almanac For the Year 1970*, p.41]

7. There is frequently a special order of experience in the life itself that for the autobiographer is inseparably linked to the discovery and invention of identity. Further, these self-defining acts may be re-enacted as the autobiographical narrative is being written. That is to say that during the process of autobiographical composition the qualities of these prototypical autobiographical acts may be re-expressed by the qualities of the act of *remembering* as distinct from or in addition to the substantive content of the *remembered* experience. The autobiographer may even be drawn to suggest in the completed narrative that such a re-enactment has taken place. Thus the act of composition may be conceived as a mediating term in the autobiographical enterprise, reaching back into the past not merely to recapture but to repeat the psychological rhythms of identity formation, and reaching forward into the future to fix the structure of this identity in a permanent self-made existence as literary text. This is to understand the writing of autobiography not merely as the passive, transparent record of an already completed self but rather as an integral and often decisive phase of the drama of self-definition. [Paul John Eakin, *Fictions in Autobiography: Studies in the Art of Self-Invention*, p.226]

TWENTY

1. A couple of years ago my mother and I were driving past
the Old Union Cemetery, which we have done dozens of
times in the last twenty years since my father died. She
glanced out the window and said quietly, as if it had just
bobbed up into her memory, Your grandfather took care
of the flowerbeds in that park. He designed all the gardens in the town parks. She looked at me as if she were
defying me to challenge this completely unexpected
piece of news. I was almost sixty years old and it was the
first time she had ever acknowledged anything about my
grandfather that could be called a virtue or merit. You've
never told me anything like that about him before, I said.
I always thought he could never hold down a job because
of his drinking. Then she became fierce, as if I were the
one who had unfairly criticized her father. Something I
still haven't been able to discover had happened to
unlock her affection for him after all the years of denial
and denunciation. Maybe something said in a conversation with her older sister Rose or maybe just a decision
she made about herself in one of the early morning sessions of remembering she has told me about. Now she
released details about my grandfather as if she were
opening a suppressed file. He had been a wonderful
mason, for example, and when they were pouring the
foundations for the Post Office the men came to the
house and insisted that Joe was the only one to mix the
cement. A family myth. My grandmother was embarrassed because he was still in bed sleeping off a drunk.
He can't come, she said, he's sick. But they knew him as
well as she did and sent a boy to the hotel for a pail of
beer and he got up and drank it and he went uptown
with them and mixed the cement. He could fix anything,
my mother says proudly, but he couldn't hold on to a job.
If he didn't feel like going in to work he just didn't go.

Nobody could depend on him, even though they liked him. He was popular, too popular, she says, rolling her eyes humorously, forgiving him without even noticing. That was when I was a little girl.

2. Dream: I'm in the lounge of the Hotel Monte Carlo in Mexico City (where cars drive through the lobby to park in back) glancing through a tattered copy of *Revista des Revistas*, a Mexican magazine that collects its materials from other magazines, waiting for Merlin to come down from the room (though I know also that Merlin was not with me in Mexico City). I begin trying to translate a poem, with difficulty, since my Spanish vocabulary is too small and I can't recognize the verb tenses, but I'm going along, something about storefronts and trees, windows, a man and a woman sipping drinks — when I suddenly recognize it as a poem I wrote a couple of years ago! It's amazing! It's about Merlin and me courting, Bloor Street in the fall of 79, the Gladstone Library. I pick it out, word by word, full of wonder. How did it get here? Who translated it? Merlin arrives and I tell her, but when I open the magazine again to show her the poem I can't find it. We both go through it page after page but it's disappeared. Then I wake up laughing and wake Merlin to tell her.

3. Work on the Town Hall and Market House continued in 1848, and the first half of 1849, but it was eventually completed; and on the evening of July 16, 1849, its Council Chamber was occupied by the Town Council for the first time. The town offices were on the first floor with an entrance on the Main Street side, and with eight stone steps leading up to the front door . . . The basement was used for butchers' stalls, and farmers' stands on each side of a long corridor which ran from an entrance door at the south end to one at the north end. Also in the basement, and reached by a door in the east wall, was the jail and Alfie Bennett's Crystal Palace Saloon. The proximity of these was very handy for the police-

man, — he had to drag drunks only a few feet. It was also handy for the Councillors who could adjourn to the basement for refreshments when all went smoothly, or could be tossed into the cells to cool off in case of a fist fight, a not too uncommon occurrence.

Outside, the Town Hall was surrounded by a broad plank walk with an adjacent ditch so that farmers coming to market could back their wagons into the ditch, and the citizens on the sidewalk could see what was in the wagons without craning their necks. High up, under the broad eaves, on all four sides were the thickly clustered clay nests of hundreds of swallows which enlivened the vicinity with their swift flittings and their gay chatterings. [*The History of the Town of Dundas, Part Three*, p.33]

4. Proust's attitude toward a writer's work is something quite particular. His masterpiece is constructed, if not on, at least in the company of, a theory of involuntary memory, of the rising to the surface of memories and sensations. This free-flowing remembrance obviously involves a kind of idleness. To be idle, within that particular perspective, is — to use the Proustian metaphor — to be like the madeleine that slowly dissolves in the mouth, which, at that moment, is idle. The subject allows himself to disintegrate through memory, and he is idle. If he were not idle, he would find himself once more in the domain of voluntary memory. [*Roland Barthes: The Grain of the Voice*, p.343]

5. Is this fiction or something I picked up from one of my colleagues: a man, associate professor, 55-ish, separated for 10 years from his wife, has intermittent relationships with two women, one an artist of 32, the other a teacher in one of the other colleges in town, no intentions of marriage, etc. What happens? The ex-wife surfaces, of course — comes back from somewhere foreign — Europe — exhausted, *depleted*, separated from another partner and totally broke. She desperately needs his help, and he

can't refuse. In fact, he is a bit excited. He lets her use his spare bedroom (really his study) until she can get started again. He thinks of her — he *thinks* he does — as "family", like a sister: their turbulent lives are far in the past. She has not aged well, looks ashen and wilted; tells him of some serious operations she has had. Her kids — 3 — from a first marriage have all but abandoned her, don't keep in touch. They don't sleep together, except in his dreams where they are both young again — 20 years ago — and full of energy and curiosity. She is not up when he leaves for work, is often out when he returns and doesn't come in until late. Where does she go? He doesn't know. She speaks vaguely of friends — oh, a woman I met in Florence, a man my partner used to do business with, a bunch of people . . . She seems to be settling in, making no plans to get a job or another place to live, bringing in more clothes. Where does her money come from? She is cool and collected when she does see him, as if it is *her* place, informs him that she'll be out, etc. and if So-and-So should call, tell him . . . etc. At first he is only amused by this, though also irritated, then begins to be furious at being taken advantage of. His artist friend and teacher friend no longer, of course, spend any nights with him, and stop inviting him to their places. They at first find him gallant to help his ex, then become suspicious, eventually impatient. This is where the story begins. He can't get rid of X, and Y and Z (who know about each other and accept the arrangement) start making things unpleasant. What? Should they insist on meeting/confronting her? Does her bland presence precipitate some gross changes in his previously settled life — thus exposing his precariousness, his depression? I think of a party they're all at — X because of another connection, not expecting him to be there, the other two starting to be a twosome themselves, getting a bit drunk and mocking him. Then what?

5. The birds at sunset over the Bay of Fundy in the summer of 1967. I sat for hours watching the huge flocks — hundreds of swallows from the honeycombed cliffs at Red Head and Blomidon's Peak — wheeling and swooping, diving towards the few bathers and then whirling straight up, turning and breaking and forming again into two or three fleets, flying headlong through each other.

> Their world breaks violently apart
> miraculously reforming
> with no shocks collisions casualities
> no mournful aftermaths
> only the reckless exhilaration
> of these voiceless brainless swifts

One day, walking out into the wide tidal flats, between the boulders huge as houses exposed at low tide, I gradually became aware of a clicking sound everywhere, like muted crickets, like some electrical short-circuit fizzzing dangerously inside my head. I couldn't find a source for it anywhere until I glanced down to the pools and slick rocks under my feet and saw thousands of snails, huge colonies clustered together, moving slightly as if with the motion of the water, harvesting the slime from the rocks. I felt shunted out to the farthest reach of my consciousness, alone on the edge of something I could just barely apprehend, like a dream warning that tantalizes the sleeper, just out of touch and then withheld, and I remember shivering with a mixture of rapture and dread that sent me hurrying back to the shore.

6. My assignment from Pearl: to take the 7-year-old I was on my knee and hug him. This because of my memory of *never* sitting on my father's knee or receiving any sign of tenderness from him — at least until his last days in hospital. Not that other boys I knew then were luckier, but

that it apparently meant so much to me: that little boy's conviction of *not counting* or of being worthless still operating and interfering with my life. Pearl: He has curled up and withdrawn, made himself inconsolable, but is still intervening with his presence in all the other activities of the other parts of the self. No use scorning him — or myself — with admonitions to be mature or sensible. "Grow up!" is not the same as "Act your age!" All these rebukes (and rebukes are what I cannot *stand*) merely confirm him in his conviction and the safety of his response to it. I am not my father. I do not have to see that little boy as dangerous or confounding. No doubt my father feared for the little boy's chances in a world he knew punished "softness", but no doubt also he was simply scared of him and turned away.

7. The sun comes through the maple tree from almost due South, and catches a hanging bunch of yellow and yellow-green leaves like a spotlight. Nothing else, except that this simple accident becomes an invitation to look at the branch, which I might otherwise not have seen.

8. **writer.** Various classifications of writers have been suggested. A frequent division is in two: (a) the man that has a story or emotion to convey, and takes the words for it; (b) the man that rouses to the feel of words, the use of language, the challenge of expression, and finds a tale to clothe with his delight. [Joseph T. Shipley, Ed. *Dictionary of World Literature*, p.452] (*The man!*)

TWENTY-ONE

1. Acceptance of three poems yesterday by *Descant* has made me happy — especially as their spokesman has instituted a policy I have been advocating for years: of praising the poems that are being accepted instead of just flatly acknowledging that they will be taken. These are for a special "FOOD" issue, so I'll send along my translation of Neruda's "Ode to Broth of Conger" as well. Read a late poem by David Ignatow the other day on waking now, these days of elderly life, fighting panic — that everyone is *separate* and no longer joined, as in families. Then the sound of birdsong from the window.

2. He was introduced to sex and sexual anticipation early, and was always excited by it, avid, ready to drop anything else without reflection, even into middle age. On Saturday afternoons at the movies when he was about 7 sitting beside his cousin Audrey, with his sister on her other side. Audrey was 12 or 13, a tall skinny girl with a round face like Olive Oyl. Sometime during those early days of her babysitting, she had taught him to put his fingers in her vulva (it was an extension of the Doctor games with Neenie) while she unbuttoned his fly and took my little erect prick in her hand and pulled at it. In the dark moviehouse they sat with their hands under their coats, spread over their laps, and touched and bumped until she said to stop. A feeling of *sweet*, like the feeling he sometimes got shimmying up and then sliding down one of the poles that supported the swings on the Public School Grounds. He must have been sworn to secrecy since he can't remember telling anyone about it. He knew that they had to make sure his sister didn't know what they did. How many Saturday afternoons did this happen? Also lying on the grass near the Cenotaph in the Old Union Cemetery, with cars passing

less than thirty feet away, thinking they were hidden by the bushes while he pushed and pulled rhythmically to Audrey's directions, sometimes it seemed for a long time, until she told him he could stop. Of course he knew it was "dirty" but the furtiveness and and anxiety and Audrey's urgency were addictive and he never really tried to avoid it. It must have gone on for a couple of years, but his memory is vague. Anyway, at some time it stopped, and when he saw Audrey at family gatherings she paid no attention to him. As he grew older he realized that others regarded her as a fool, retarded even. She had failed both Grade Four and Grade Five once each, and like the big boys at the back of the Grade Six class had waited out her time until she could legally leave school. A few years later she married a man as silly as herself who worked at a gas station and the pair of them were always happy and silly whenever he saw them, clowning even at funerals.

3. "What is the use of being a little boy if you are to be a man what is the use." [Gertrude Stein, *Everybody's Autobiography*, p. 133]

4. The longest lived newspaper in Dundas has been the STAR, which is still publishing today (1968) in its 78th year. As previously recorded, the Dundas STANDARD ceased publication Oct. 4, 1890 and was purchased by A.R. Wardell and T.B. Townsend, who hired John Fry of the STANDARD staff to be their Editor. The new owners wished to change the name of the paper but had no large type other than the few letters in the name STANDARD. In this quandary Mr. Fry suddenly thought of the name STAR which could be formed by merely using four of the letters of the old name STANDARD, consequently the reborn paper was christened, "The Dundas STAR" with the subsidiary name, "AND WENT-WORTH NEWS RECORD" added in smaller letters. [*The History of the Town of Dundas*, Part 3, p.67]

5. His family never cared about records except in incom-
   plete snapshot albums and endlessly disputed anecdotes.
   Sequences of family history tended to break down early
   as some random item distracted the teller, and then one
   item reminded somebody of another item from a different time, even concerning a different person (maybe
   proving that So-and-so was like his uncle after all,
   though you'd never think it to look at them or hear them
   talk). This is oral time, structured by digression, stretch-
   ing out in all directions, into the future as easily as into
   the past. For people like his family maybe so much
   eludes any useful (or usable) language that it becomes as
   if it doesn't happen, hasn't happened. The stories don't
   get told, the cousins do not talk about the grandparents
   they share, and so much of what might have been said is
   simply — not repressed, that would be too active a form
   of what I mean — just not registered, not raised to the
   surface of words, but left buried somewhere in feelings.
   Anger, bitterness, shame, fear, regret, the unrecorded history of people of the bottom class who don't respect their
   lives. Like his mother they didn't want to remember.
   They needed to forget what still threatened to drag them
   down. What they needed to pretend to others and to
   each other was not really so. To be clean, to eat decent
   food, to pay your debts, to have a good time now and
   then, wasn't that enough? But there was something
   wrong about an aunt's death, oh years ago, when she was
   a girl of eighteen. Something suspicious, unsavory. And
   wasn't her inheritance just stolen by that other branch of
   the family? She was a pretty girl, an orphan really, living
   with her stepmother when she died. Or maybe she was
   housekeeping then for somebody, some doctor in
   Hamilton?

6. At the Y each morning after writing I stretched and rode
   a stationary bicycle and sometimes swam. Sometimes I

continued to think about what I had been writing into the journal, but usually I fell into a kind of trance, settling into the rhythms of my body like the dozen or so other regulars who made up the clan or family of early morning exercisers. We greeted each other with waves and grunts, hardly knowing each other's names, but reassured to see each other all the same. For a couple of months one winter two pregnant women swam at the same time every morning, moving slowly and smoothly up and down the lanes together, their bellies bulging more every time I saw them. I kept trying to get up my nerve to ask them how the babies enjoyed their swims, but never managed to do it.

7. Writing *is* the possibility of change. Who said that? Might have been Duras in one of those mock interviews (to pass the time). The point is that it works not only for the person sitting at the terminal typing away without knowing what comes next but for the reader too, catching the hints of a new direction, a sidelong glance that changes everything. In the barthesian sense too — it might have been/might be different, multiple, not what was intended. Duras keeps saying, You might put it differently, although she claims not to like Barthes. I don't have a story of my life, I have writing that I do when I confront or accept my ignorance about life. *C'est pour passer le temps.*

TWENTY-TWO

1. Edward Hopper's "Night Hawks". They're poised in one of those long silences in which nobody speaks, though they each feel that they might be just about to, and they are all listening, or ready to listen — but at the same time they are all comfortable with each other and the place and time. They are lingering, reluctant to bring an end to the mood — to enter the next stage of something, even if it's only the next stage of the night before morning and the necessity of getting up and going to work. For this long moment they're a family, a tribe, these few people — one of whom has not spoken for forty minutes — all sharing a single compound consciousness. Inside: color, warmth, good smells, company; outside: empty streets, thick twilight, lonely insomnia. It seems like a good place to stay.

   Across the street from the diner Hopper has let the light project on the walls of a building. Unlikely, as is the greenish, yellowish color of the sidewalk outside the window (the green repeated from inside). A curved window (unlikely?) at the corner. The scene is familiar — in experience and memory and movies. All the light/color leaking outside establishes the diner as haven, life — just as the red hair and dress and man's face, and in the counter top too (whose interior shape repeats the wedge-shape of white/yellow at the top inside of the diner) — and across the street the 2nd storey wall punctuated by the dark windows (there are two triangles of light over there, one upstairs and one downstairs in the store front; but there is also a shadow that looks as if it ought to go from the frame post of this store window over the triangle of light. What's the source of that light? And why is it only in *one* of the windows upstairs?

Apparently there's a conversation between the couple and the counterman, but the solitary man — dressed, it seems, identically to the man of the couple — has his back to the viewer and seems to be looking into the middle distance, lonely, depressed, or maybe just dreamy. At least he is solitary. The painting is filled with values — the dark/light spectrum which puts a frame, almost, around the interior scene — like a stage set, and the middle-tones outside that almost refuse to represent anything. The number of repetitions.. A couple sits together with a single man (the counterman) nearby — and the two metal coffee urns sit together with a blank door near them. The fedoras of the men. (I was 10 when this was painted, my father like most men you saw on the street wore a fedora, though his prize hat was the pearl gray Homburg with a soft crease down the middle that he wore when he was dressed up to go to the Ladies' Beverage Room at the Collins Hotel) The stools are repeated and the shape of white coffee mugs, windows (repositories of emptiness — nothing is ever really *in* a window; rather, a window is a shape imposed on a subject), the empty windows across the street (stage-set, slightly too-small street) blank, a couple even half-lidded — eyes, lenses, looking at the scene from the other side.

Triangles or wedge shapes — the wedge of yellow at the top of the interior scene as the wall continues across the far window to a point just under the facade. (Question: how do you get *into* this diner? Oh, no doubt there's a door out of sight on the right, but no other door, at the corner or at the other end of the counter? This is a dream diner.) Directly under this, facing in the other direction, at the bottom left of the painting, the wedge shape again, as the sidewalk is cropped for the frame. Then — at the very top, when the building across the street ends, a small triangle/wedge of black and under that the continuation of the Phillies sign into another wedge. Across the street the light (*from where?*) in the store window that contains a ghostly cash register takes the shape of a triangle/wedge and is repeated in an upstairs window. More and more — like one of those Sunday Paper puzzles for children: Find all the monkeys in this picture.

John Berger, in *Looking at Pictures*, claims to scorn this kind of displacing of affective response into technical execution, values etc., but what's the problem? Consider: although you might be lonely in this city/town it is remarkably clean (again like a stage set, dream set) and all in all, that is balancing the emptiness and solitariness — the abstraction of the shapes and values — with the casual intimacy of the couple and the friendly exchange (apparently) between customers and counterman this is a warm, romantic, humanistic picture — the diner takes the place of a shrine, say, where certain values are located, where one can go for company. It's cheap, clean, familiar, friendly, and it's *available* when everything else is closed and empty. Hemingway would recognize this as a "clean, well-lighted place" (the date is easily accomodating, though I know nothing about Hopper's reading).

The shapes are also full of comfort and relief — the big rectangles, rectangles *within* rectangles — and the slabs of dark in the long shadowed sections of the outside wall, the façade of the diner. Then the colors and the contrasts of the colors — the woman's red dress echoes in the red-brown of the counter, and in the red-orange of the building across the street. And — the *green* of the narrow band, the trim, around the bottom of the window, running up the window frame twice, and washed paler on the sidewalk — green (especially balancing out that yellow and the light brown door and red).

Surfaces — cruising them — gorgeous text that never stops *saying* — deconstructing its codes incessantly — a good poem that tells you, *It felt good to do this!*

TWENTY-THREE

1. December evening driving home from the bakery with a fruit-and-flan pie for dinner guests from Holland. A man lies face down in the crosswalk at Dovercourt, not moving. I stopped my car (horns from the drivers behind me who can't see) and helped him up, a man my age well dressed in a blue overcoat, plump, red-faced. I broke my glasses, he says, holding them up, one wing in the wrong hand. Make sure you're okay, I said. You could be in shock. Did you bump your head? I was holding him by the arm. He wants to get away. I thought how easily he could be me, embarrassment the worst problem. No, no, I'm not in shock, he said, I'm just drunk. He was smiling my Uncle Bert's quick smile of unrepentence. It's a bad night to be drunk, too slippery. But I'll manage, thanks. I don't have far to go now. Thank you for your help. And he totters off across College Street toward the YMCA, one of the respectable drunks of our neighborhood where usually they travel in pairs, turn up knobby broken faces to ask for change. It was my birthday. Two days ago I had seen Wim Wenders' movie *Wings of Desire* about the sad angels whispering into despondent ears or hugging lonely suicides — and envying humans so much, their intensities of feeling, their world of small distractions. The man in the blue overcoat was one of them, wandering the streets in search of those of us who needed this other comfort. Then home to dinner with Barbara and Bas, where the conversation moved to friends who had ended their lives alone.

2. I always wanted Layton to write poems about ageing. Not ga ga but angry with some wisdom finally. There's so much bumf about the old, fierce old fanatics and protesters "still full of life" or cute old clowns laughing about their sex drives. What about the sore mouths

when dentures have to be replaced — again! — or blood in the stool or no stool for days? I like the snappishness sometimes — right to the point, are you dying or not. The ones who don't care what they eat, live on toast for weeks, or where they go if anywhere, though they lie about this not to lose the company they crave. Wake in the night, "bad thoughts, bad thoughts", no use to anybody. "I'll be in Heaven soon, what do I care about *this* shit?" They know they're moving into a zone beyond which no one will ever take them seriously again. So what? The nurse wants to know, How're we doing today? Tell her for once.

3. In 1844, a book entitled "The Emigrant to North America" was published in England with this comment on Dundas: "After passing through Dundas, a neat village buried in a valley I ascended the mountain where I got a view of remarkable beauty, — the valley between this and the village of Ancaster. I have seldom if ever seen anything of its kind to equal it." This still hold true. It is one of our Town's greatest assets. Why not make more look-out points? [*The History of the Town of Dundas, Part Three, p.13*]

4. Is it the patience of horses? My childhood memories are of many delivery horses — breadman, milkman, butcher — and of their great weariness, sorrow, and patience. They stood heavily, with their heads low, as low as the harness would allow, and they walked with what seemed an unnecessary accompaniment of muscles and joints for the amount of terrain covered or the speed maintained. They plodded a few steps, stopped while a delivery was made, then a few more. Some I especially admired (the milkman's?) were able to go on by themselves as deliveries were made down the whole street. Then the milkman — Bob Hunt! — would whistle and the horse would come up to where he was standing and wait while he emptied his wire basket of empties and put in more full

bottles. I suppose the horses I saw were old, or middle-aged. Even Frank Crump's or Rab Dunning's farm horses, strong and energetic as they were. I don't remember specifically young horses anyway until I was in my teens and going out to the Palomino Ranch with Patty to ride by the hour.

The horse, the horse. The way lips curl back to bare the huge teeth when you offer a horse an apple or a carrot. The whuff of hot wet air through the round nostrils. Generally, like some breeds of dogs, the messiness horse-lovers have to put up with — slobber, especially when a horse tosses its head unexpectedly, or lays it over your shoulder or nuzzles your chest. You pat a horse on the nose, and then what do you do with your hand?

5. As for the sacred outline, I admit having sacrificed at its altars during a certain period in the beginnings of semiology. Since then there has been that whole movement challenging the dissertation and its format. My university experience has also shown me the very oppressive, not to say repressive, constraints brought to bear upon students by the myth of the outline and syllogistic Aristotelian development (this was even one of the problems we attempted to examine this year in my seminar). In short, I opted for an aleatory cutting-up, a *découpage* (into what I call "miniatures"). My aim is to deconstruct the dissertation, to deflate the reader's anxiety, and to reinforce the critical part of writing by fracturing the very notion of the "subject" of a book. [Roland Barthes, *The Grain of the Voice*,181-2]

6. The charm of publications by small town historical societies. I love them as much for their faults as for their dedicated preservation of minute facts and ideologies. I read them avidly, but randomly, since they can't help but be

constructed in fragments and hiatuses, my favorite kind
of text, and I wish their writers — those spinsters of good
family and retired school principals and lawyers —
would feel freer to let themselves go more in their irre-
pressible enthusiasms and disapprovals and their convic-
tions of the blessedness of their undertaking. Maybe
nothing is better for invoking that familiar nostalgia of a
town's children who escaped early and for good to a larger world and always wondered if in fact their escape was
really part of a subtle expulsion of misfits by which the
town kept its official life unblemished by skepticism or
hard scrutiny. For the writers of these accounts all "old"
or "prominent" families are unspotted, patriarchs noble
as well as ambitious, ladies gracious and full of good
deeds. Whatever is, is good, even better maybe when the
writer herself has only shared the culture of the town's
rich and powerful on sufferance. I'm straying. I meant
to express my pleasure in reading of places and sometimes people who strangely — in this flow of small town
events — still mattered to my own life there in the 1930's
and '40's, and daydreaming of what went on in the
unrecorded events or suppressed pages of the scattered
records. (*Where is my grandfather, "Smokey" Joe Wood?*) I
see now that if it is a kind of nostalgia that moves me here
it is also the still helpless rage of the unempowered at
being offered such an "official" lifestory without the
means to complain. The maddening complacency of
these accounts! The story is always the same and it is
always for me a variation on the Presbyterian rewarding
of prudence and good manners, and the avidity of the
governed to assume the values of the governing and to
punish their own faltering brothers and sisters. (Brother!
Where am I going with this? The lingo throws me back
to Sunday School in the '40's and my eager reading of
Anglo-Catholic recruiters when I was in High School.)

Here's a short anthology of fragments from the commentary on 214 Park St. W. in *Picturesque Dundas Update*, published by the Dundas Historical Museum in 1981: When members of one family stay in a house for more than sixty years, there must be something in the old saying 'home is where the heart is' . . . His kindly disposition, keen sense of humour and practical wisdom won for him public confidence to an unusual degree . . . He later moved to the large house built by John Forsyth (192 Governor's Road) which he called 'Uplands'. Today it is known as 'Ballindalloch'. . . .James Somerville, who never lost interest in his boyhood home on Park St. W., died May 24th, 1916 at his own home 'Uplands', and so Dundas lost at that time, her oldest native-born resident. One of the highly respected men across our Dominion, it is people like James Somerville who help to shape the destiny of a country . . . This home has an enviable history of families enjoying it so much, they don't want to leave. The Somervilles were there for 63 years and to date, the Finlayson family for 64 years. Truly an outstanding and unusual record.

What bothers me about this silly stuff? I'm thrown back into adolescence. My mix of scorn and frustration is what used to drive me wild with the adults in charge when I was 16.

7. Still dark. The trees just barely appear, dark shapes against darker ones. I can see my neighbors in their bright french windows. They're dressed early this morning. The child in his snowsuit walks back and forth trailing his long scarf on the floor. His (?) mother has no time for makeup today, her husband is already in the car and the brake lights come on at the end of the lane and the house lights are out again. Just now over the houses a long band of color — purple, pink, then a kind of yellow that blends gradually into blue.

8. Text of pleasure: the text that contents, fills, grants euphoria; the text that comes from culture and does not break with it, is linked to a *comfortable* practice of reading. Text of bliss: the text that imposes a state of loss, the text that discomforts (perhaps to the point of a certain boredom), unsettles the reader's historical, cultural, psychological assumptions, the consistency of his tastes, values, memories, brings to crisis his relation with language. [Roland Barthes, *The Pleasure of the Text*, 14]

TWENTY-FOUR

1. The garden is a made bed. I am trying to get a word in. Turn down the covers. Move along. This is an old story. Don't put it down. I am for the moment. Keep missing. I must draw the line somewhere. The batter lined out to right field. The next one hit a line drive single through the infield. Falling into line. A hair line crack. In the morning check the tide line. The poet has been setting out his lines overnight. Seasoning. Anyone intending to dig should check for buried, hidden lines underground. Keep it in mind. I'll re mind you. First the out line. Think again. Blooming flowers. You could have fooled me. What crossed your mind?

2. "Many years ago, when in business in Dundas I thought the affairs of the province were not rightly managed," he said, "and although I knew nothing of printing, I felt I had something to say to the public, so I engaged a printer, and started a newspaper. I have not come here," he said, "to defend all that I said, and all that I have done, but I would say that I wished to do right, at any rate. I wanted to see Canada flourish. My life has been a chequered one, and I hope some good may yet come of it." [From a *Dundas WARDER* report of an election meeting in the Town Hall, March 15, 1851, at which former resident and business man William Lyon Mackenzie spoke in connection with his second attempt to win the election as Member of the Provincial Parliament for Haldimand. He won both elections, though he was unseated the first time by his opponents as having defective qualifications. *The History of the Town of Dundas, Part Two*, p.33]

3. This assignment from Pearl: to write to the Great Nothingness that I have feared since childhood — and that overcame me again last night. It hits me first physically, a lurch or a shudder and an actual feeling of physical debility in the stomach and back. Like flu, something I can seem to taste without being able to identify it. I

hold myself still to see if I can take it, like unexpected pain — though it *isn't* pain, exactly — and to shrink myself around it, make myself fit it precisely. And immediately or at the same time a wave of despair goes through me like a long wail of anguish. I am absolutely alone and without power or any prospect of power, or even the possibility of survival. *Something* is about to happen. *Is happening.* It can't be stopped or avoided. This time it will overcome me, just destroy me. I will just not be. Not even that I will be attacked and destroyed, but just that, impersonally, conditions will not *include* me. Immediately I recognize this as the old feeling, familiar since childhood, and from vivid memories of my teens, later at University, all through my first two marriages — the devastating fear of total irrelevance, total worthlessness. I can't get past this moment, except by the reminder (and how early did *this* begin?) that I have got past it before and that I only have to hold myself tight and wait for it to go or release me or pass on for now. This time not the final time. It needs no explanation or cause, it is self-evident, an absolute condition which has always been and that makes its presence known periodically without warning. *When?* With it, fear, shame. In order of experience the shame of having it appear again, of having no defence, of being too weak, of being captive, slave — and then its inherent shame that goes back beyond comprehension to shame that my lifesecurity can be so fragile as if this were a sign of inherent inferiority, like feeblemindedness. The fear also that the imminent collapse of whatever appearance of stability there might be was already expected by others (read: *adults*) who saw through the false conformism of *my* adults to the hatred and betrayal and disgust they accused and defended each other with. If what they said to each other was true — and how much of this, for a child, was tone of voice and facial expression and physical gesture? — then they were both depraved and loathsome. But — they would not be so — or would not be saying these things if it weren't for me and my sister. They fought because of us. Not what we did but *that we were.* And then the complication of this, that my mother, and *her* mother, were spoiling us, had already spoiled *me,* a cry-baby. And that my father couldn't stand to spend one minute with us because he had no feelings. The shame of this. If anyone else should hear it, know of it. Their disgust and pity and contempt. So I must have started early introjecting these implacable judges who still condemn me.   Like a hot surge through my middle making me curl and hug myself and wail or sob, at least internally: *Oh, no! Not again! NOT NOW!* Nothing to redeem me from this NOTHING that I am and that I am in.   I have no resources but simple endurance, just to wait it out, and when it passes, forget it and go on with the parts of my life that are safe and neutral and won't attract this . . . what, *punishment?* For what? Being myself.

Pearl says, What next?   Suppose I have my usual resources about me the next time this NOTHING appears, how would they begin to cope, what are their skills along this line. Or she says, what happens if you talk to NOTHING as a *person* rather than a condition, say, What's going on here, what's this all about, what the devil are you trying to do? Etc. Somewhere there was a *purpose* for it, something meant for my good, or my protection. Something some child dreamed up. Time now to say, I don't need this any more, I figured out how to handle things without it, it's just in the way now, let it drop.

4. Sitting on the deck since 6:30 under the maple tree (since removed furiously by ten men working at top speed until midnight the day I drove in from work to discover that I could see *through* its trunk — split mortally after a wind

storm).   Reading some of the other articles in the *Hemingway Review* that has my article on *In Our Time*. Curiously pleasant feeling of community: we all write away at these things in private, working out our obsessions about the texts, and then come together in the *Review* as if speaking to each other, trying to *persuade* each other. Instead of writing lately, the early mornings are so fine, I've been reading, mostly trying to catch up on theory.

Thinking a lot about writing prose, the pleasure of sheer bulk, pouring in details and then dwelling on them, telling details to somebody directly, as if begged by the reader not to leave anything out, please. Also, of course, as I think of pages of text unreeling I think that putting down one sentence, describing or mentioning one detail means that others must be omitted, and that accumulating these arbitrary (seemingly arbitrary) bits is the way text gets itself written, a historical record of omissions. The distractions out here on the deck. Noisy sparrows in their lovemaking, a robin singing the same phrase over and over, the squirrels playing (screwing?), the grackles trying to fit themselves on the narrow perches and reach into the feeders designed for small birds. Yesterday I typed into the PC some remarks from a curious review of *Heavy Horse Judging* by Martin Singleton (do I know him?): hated most of the book, he said, but he kept quoting it all over the place. I guess he'd really hate the new MS (shall it be *Remembering Sleep* or *naditas*?). Wants "stronger endings," meaning closure, meaning confidence, meaning Signifieds. When I came out here this morning a thin band of sunlight cut up the backyard two houses north, while all the east was in shadow. The sun came directly and precisely between two houses on the next street, like something at Stonehenge, something with a special significance.

5. List of *"Remarkable Days"*, May 1 to 31, 1979, from *Baer's Agricultural Almanac*: *Philip & James*, Sigismund, *Inv.of Cross*, Florianus, Godard, Aggeus, Domicella, Stanislaus, Job, Gorianus, Mamertus, Pancratius, *Mothers' Day*, Christianus, Sophia, Perigrinus, Joducus, *Peace Day, Armed Forces*, Torpetus, Hosditius, *Nat. Maritime*, Desiderius, *Ascension Day*, Urbanus, Edward, Luciaus, *Memorial Day*,Maxmilian, Beitzel, Manilius.

6. We drove hard for three days to get to the PowWow at Rapid City. After, we went north and west, up through the Black Hills and Dakatoh country (signed everywhere as Custer Country: Custer Motel, Custer Bar and Restaurant, Custer National Park) and farther, up to Saskatchewan and the Cypress Hills around Eastend and the Cypress Hills National Park. Red Cloud and Sitting Bull. At the Crazy Horse memorial, down the road from Mt. Rushmore, once a day the sons of the original money-maker-entrepreneur-Indian-lover-artist set off a stick or two of dynamite for the tourists on the Welcome Center beside the store; you can look through a telescope at the unfinished sculpture — the *mountain!* — of Crazy Horse riding forward into the unclouded sky. At Wounded Knee, markers for the American soldiers, a whole field of crosses. On a radio station from the Reservation a young woman discussed Infant Alcohol Syndrome. This country, like the Badlands, is reluctant to co-operate with tourists, withholds itself. It prefers to be empty, ignores your presence, discourages with an absence of thought-forms. You may look until it fills you with itself. A waiting. An energy.

7. Hemingway's curious play with the paradigm SOMETHING/NOTHING/ANYTHING/EVERYTHING. "The End of Something" certainly, and "Hills Like Green Elephants" and "A Clean, Well-Lighted Place". Others. The terms migrate

across the borders of the separate stories and novels to establish a kind of intermittent misgiving of the language — that is, comprehensible and unremarkable in their contexts as realistic or mimetic signs, the words also set up a kind of distraction from themselves as part of the paradigm: if "nothing" comes, can "everything" be far behind? In textual terms this behavior of the language promotes delay and deferring of meaning assignments indefinitely — no matter how loudly or insistently some readers will claim to "know what it means". This is not the issue. Of course we know what it means: it inscribes a code or formula that is always/already understood. But what does it *do* when it is not "meaning"? (Or, what is it doing when . . . etc.). Like other patterns of repetition in *In Our Time* this one has a function of insisting on the primacy of text, of *écriture*, the author-less text that does not represent or express but keeps us perpetually reminded that all representation and expression are accessible only through the medium which will not say (only) what we wish it to say (*mean* it to say). Nothingeverythingsomethinganything, along with all-right and the others sets up a peculiar kind of disturbance that not only undermines our confidence in understanding the meaning (or in meanings that can be understood) but that persistently insinuates the terms of existential distress that Camus admired so much in Hemingway.

8. November 1990/1996. Enough leaves have fallen that I can see across the backyards to the family I watched last winter in the mornings: mother and father and one small child, walking back and forth across the French windows in progressive stages of dress and preparation for their day. Then lights out and the red glow as the car moved out of the driveway. I depended on them for company, imagined personalities for them, scenarios for their occa-

sional conversations (or, from this distance, mimes of conversation) and embraces. Then as spring came and summer the leaves grew too thick to peer through. Now they are about to return. I wonder what they have been doing over the summer. Has the baby grown? Have they got new wardrobes. Do the adults still meet sometimes in the hall for a quick kiss before rushing off to find a shirt, some socks, the sweater they want? Where did they go for their holidays? I hope somewhere warm and friendly. All winter I worried, their coats looked so thin, even from here I could see them shiver. I think they would like to buy a dog, for the child — is it a boy or a girl? — but they'd have to leave it all day, a dog's life. He is a lawyer, she teaches, why not? Every day I waited for their lights and watched their distant shapes cross the windows, pause in the kitchen for juice, a slice of toast, half a cup of coffee, then out into their Toronto. Maybe some morning I could get up a little earlier, waylay them, thank them for their amazing assurance of the next moment, next day.

di.ur.nal (dī ûr´ nàl), *adj.* **1.** of or pertaining to each day; daily. **2.** of or pertaining to the daytime. **3.** *Bot.* showing a periodic alteration of condition with day and night, as certain flowers which open by day and close by night. **4.** active by day, as certain birds and insects. — *n.* **5.** *Liturgy.* a service book containing the offices for the day hours of prayer. **6.** *Archaic.* a diary. [*t. LL: s. diurnālis* daily]

di.ur.nal pa.ral.lax (pà´ rà lăks´). *n.* the displacement of a body owing to its being observed from the surface instead of from the center of the earth.

Writing and reading or writing/reading, the production of text: a potentially unending process which stops only through the convenience or exhaustion of the writer/ reader

Don Summerhayes was born in the Town of Dundas, in Southern Ontario. He has published four collections of poetry: *Winter Apples* (1982), *Heavy Horse Judging* (1987), *Watermelon* (1992), and *Remembering Sleep* (1993), and in 1995 was named winner of the Stephen Leacock Poetry Prize for his poem, "Lines Before My Sixty-third Birthday." Don's photographs, poems, and prose text have appeared in many Canadian Magazines. Before retiring, he taught at York University for many years. He is married to the artist and healer Merlin Homer who is also his co-editor at Deor Editions.